Snake in the Brass

Jennifer Lamont Leo

Mountain Majesty Media

Snake in the Brass

Published by Mountain Majesty Media, Inc.

PO Box 638, Cocolalla, Idaho 83813

ISBN: 979-8-9937139-0-8 (e-book)
ISBN: 979-8-9937139-1-5 (paperback)
ISBN: 979-8-9937139-2-2 (audio)

Cover design by Dee Dee Book Covers

This is a work of fiction. Names, characters, and incidents are all products of the author's imagination or are used for fictional purposes. Any mentioned brand names, places, and trade marks remain the property of their respective owners, bear no association with the author or the publisher, and are used for fictional purposes only.

Scripture quotations are taken from the King James Version (KJV).

Printed in the United States of America

Chapter One

Timber Coulee, Idaho. October 1920

The blaring trumpet that jolted me from sleep at one thirty-seven a.m. was not part of my usual routine. I bolted upright, heart hammering against my ribs, as syncopated rhythms and wailing saxophones assaulted me from downstairs.

Had I fallen asleep in a speakeasy? Not that Timber Coulee had any speakeasies—none that I knew of, anyway, though I suspected something sketchy might be going on behind the cheerful striped awnings of the ice cream parlor. Despite the store's earnest advertisements, some of the men I'd seen lurking around there didn't strike me as the type to get excited about cherry phosphates.

Bewildered, I fumbled in the dark for my robe, stumbled downstairs, and found Molly in the brightly lit kitchen, still in her Nile-green party dress, conducting an invisible orchestra with a butter knife. In the parlor, Moxie, the orange tabby, perched above the secondhand gramophone, batting at it with a delicate paw.

I marched to the infernal machine and twisted the volume down to a civilized level. A grinning reptile on the record label mocked my displeasure.

"Oh! I didn't hear you come down," Molly said when I returned to the kitchen.

"I should think not." I reached for the steaming teakettle. "Honestly. The Midnight Serpents? You realize their name doesn't dictate the hour you must listen to them?"

She buttered what appeared to be her third piece of toast, judging from the crusts on her plate. At twenty-two, my niece could eat like a farmhand while maintaining a Gloria Swanson figure—a talent I'd lost around my thirtieth birthday.

"Sorry. I didn't realize it was that loud." She plunged her knife into the jam jar.

I poured myself a cup of tea, grateful for the warmth. Then I joined her at the table. Moxie jumped onto my lap, happy for the unexpected company. "Did you have fun at Myrtle's birthday party?"

"And how! It was the bee's knees. Myrt has a swell collection of jazz records, and we really cut a rug. And guess what everyone's talking about? The concert this weekend! Think of it. The Midnight Serpents right here in Timber Coulee. Can you imagine anything more ripping?"

I could indeed, but didn't say so. "It's been a while since a good traveling show came to town. Not since before the war."

Her expression radiated pity for my lack of rippingness. "The Midnight Serpents are innovative artists," she said with exaggerated patience. Then she set her toast on a plate. "We simply must invite them to dinner when they arrive. Please say yes."

I nearly choked on my tea. "The entire band? This cottage is hardly suitable—"

"That's exactly why we should! They're probably tired of restaurant food. A home-cooked meal would be such a kindness."

"Sweetie, we don't even know these men. It would hardly be proper to—"

"But I do know one of them! Norman Walsh—the saxophonist. We were at the conservatory together." Her eyes shone. "He's the berries! So talented and such a gentleman."

This was news to me. "You never mentioned knowing anyone in the band."

"I only just realized from the posters." She grew wistful. "He probably thinks I'm terribly provincial, giving up my education to work in a small-town music shop. If he's thought of me at all."

"Your choices have been perfectly sensible."

"Norm's living the artistic life I abandoned. All the more reason to show him small-town life has its rewards! A home-cooked dinner, good conversation, friendly hospitality."

I looked around our modest kitchen. "These musicians are probably accustomed to fine hotels—"

"That's why they'd appreciate something authentic. Think how copacetic it would be for them to experience the Real McCoy."

Copacetic, indeed. Her enthusiasm was infectious, but I clung to practicality. "How many band members?"

"Five, I think."

"Five! We'd have to use the parlor and kitchen, and even then, we could scarcely seat nine people—you, me, James, Clarence, and five musicians." We could hardly leave our gentlemen friends out in the cold.

"We could borrow chairs from the church. Oh, and I could make Grandma Parrish's roast! Musicians appreciate good grub like anyone else."

"Are you certain Norman would remember you fondly enough to accept?"

"Of course! We were quite good friends." Her cheeks pinked. "Not romantically—just fellow students who shared a love of music. But he respected my abilities."

My niece's excitement seemed in danger of overshadowing even her upcoming wedding preparations. "This means a great deal to you, doesn't it?"

"It's a chance to show Norman that leaving the conservatory doesn't mean I've given up on music. I could tell him I teach violin, in addition to working at Mountain Melodies."

Something in my chest fluttered at her obvious admiration for this man, and concern for what he thought, but I dismissed it as natural nostalgia. After all, she was happily engaged to Clarence Butterworth. The wedding was set for early December, less than two months away.

Curiosity about this Norman fellow won over my objections. "I suppose we could extend the invitation. Though don't be disappointed if they decline."

"They'll accept," Molly said with absolute confidence. "Artists appreciate homespun hospitality."

I stifled a yawn, pushed Moxie from my lap, and set my teacup in the sink. "Much as I love these late-night talks, sweetie, we both have work tomorrow."

"I'm too excited to sleep. This will be such fun!"

I smiled at her enthusiasm, even if I didn't quite share it. Something about her eagerness troubled me in a way I couldn't quite define.

Chapter Two

A few hours later, the morning sun peeked through the kitchen windows as I cracked eggs into the skillet. Moxie lapped water from his dish on the floor. Molly sat at the table in her blue bathrobe.

I slid scrambled eggs onto her plate. "After dancing until all hours, you need proper nourishment."

"I had trouble sleeping." She stabbed at the fluffy yellow curds with her fork. "I've been thinking about jazz. I think it's good for Timber Coulee to be shaken up a little by an avant-garde art form."

"Is that what we're calling it?"

Before she could retort, three sharp raps echoed from the front door. We exchanged glances. Nobody called this early unless something was wrong.

"I'll get it." I wiped my hands and hurried through the parlor.

My older sister, Kathleen, stood on the porch in her navy wool traveling coat, gripping a worn carpetbag in one hand and a leather valise in the other. Her sun-bronzed skin and silver-streaked brown hair looked severe beneath a black hat.

Confusion jolted my core. "Kathleen! What are you doing here? What's happened? Is Homer—"

"Homer's fine, though he near pitched a fit when I told him I was coming early." She swept past me into the parlor and set down her valise with a decided *thunk*. Moxie sauntered over and sniffed it while Kathleen tugged off her gloves, her hands showing the evidence of years of farm work—capable, callused, strong.

I kissed her cheek, cool from the autumn chill. "We weren't expecting you until Thanksgiving."

"Plans change." She removed her hat and coat and hung them on the coat rack.

"Mother?" Molly appeared in the kitchen doorway, still clutching her fork. Her brown curls had escaped their pins, creating a halo around her face. "Is Dad with you?"

Kathleen's sturdy arms wrapped her daughter in a hug. "No, he's home attending to the farm. He'll come along later. But I couldn't wait another minute."

"Wait for what?"

"My dear, you're so thin! Doesn't Amanda feed you?" Before I could protest, Kathleen gripped Molly's shoulders and stepped back. "Good heavens, child. Past seven and you're still in your nightclothes? A wife rises before her husband to ensure his day begins properly." She marched to the kitchen, with Molly and me trailing in her wake like chastened schoolchildren.

Trying to reassert some control in my own home, I pulled out a chair. "Sit. Would you care for eggs?"

"No, thank you. Ate on the train."

She examined the cluttered counter—eggshells, abandoned butter knife, coffee grounds. Her lips pursed tighter with each discovery.

"This confirms my worst fears. I see I haven't arrived a moment too soon."

"Too soon for what?" I asked.

"That girl needs proper instruction before taking a husband." She pointed at Molly. "A woman who can't manage a household has no business getting married. From what I've read between the lines in her letters, she couldn't boil water without burning it."

As Molly stood open-mouthed, I rushed to defend her. "It's not as bad as all that." True, my niece had heretofore shown little interest in the domestic arts. But she did like to cook on occasion, and could follow a recipe. "In fact, she's gotten quite good at Mama's pot roast."

Kathleen waved aside my spirited defense. "Not your fault, Amanda."

I hadn't said that it was.

She barreled on. "A lifelong spinster couldn't be expected to teach a girl the finer points of running a home. No doubt you spend more time down at that little shop of yours than you do here in the kitchen."

A sharp response formed in my throat, but I swallowed it down. Her statement wasn't inaccurate.

"You've been living like a pampered guest, Miss Molly Mulroney. I'm here to provide proper domestic training. We'll start with cleaning and laundry, move to cooking, then household management." Kathleen rolled up her sleeves as if intending to launch the first lesson at that very moment.

"But I have to go to work," Molly protested.

The clock on the wall agreed. "She's right. We have a busy day."

"The home is your work now." Kathleen's eyes locked on Molly's. "Clarence Butterworth deserves a wife who won't disgrace his name."

Molly's jaw jutted forward—a sure signal of rising temper.

I touched her shoulder. "Run upstairs and get dressed, sweetie. We'd best be on our way. Callan mentioned instruments from the marching band that need repair before Saturday's football game."

When she'd bolted upstairs, I faced my sister. "Happy as we are to see you, I wish you'd given advance notice."

Kathleen gave a dismissive wave. "Family doesn't wait for an invitation. Besides, a well-run home is always fit for company."

"How much time are we talking about for these, er, lessons?" My voice came out meeker than intended.

"However long it takes. Only seven weeks until the wedding."

Seven weeks. A sense of panic seasoned with guilt rose in my chest. Guilt won. Her words about family not needing an invitation nagged at me. *You do for family,* our mother always said. This was my sister, after all.

I hoisted her valise. "You'll have to bunk with me. Molly's room is too small." I led the way, cringing at my unmade bed, and shoved my clothing aside in the closet.

"You can hang things here. I'll clear a dresser drawer after work. I'm sure you'd like to rest after your journey."

But Kathleen had already pulled out an apron. "I'm not a bit tired, and I aim to make myself useful."

"We'll be home shortly after six." I paused at the doorway. "I hate to leave you alone after you've just arrived."

"Don't worry about me," she said. "I'll have plenty to keep me busy."

Sure, she did. That's what made me nervous.

Chapter Three

The crisp autumn air nipped at our cheeks as Molly and I stepped onto Elm Street, our breath forming small clouds in the morning chill. I pulled my wool jacket tighter, grateful for the warm gloves she'd knitted me the previous Christmas. *See?* I thought to Kathleen. *The girl's not completely undomesticated.*

Moxie strolled ahead, ready to put in a full day of sunbeam-lounging. Trudging beside me, Molly was uncharacteristically silent.

"Well, this is an unexpected turn of events," I said as cheerfully as I could.

"I won't let her spoil things."

"What things?"

"This weekend. The concert. The dinner with the Serpents. Everything."

In the confusion, I'd forgotten about Friday's potential guests. "We haven't asked them yet," I ventured with caution, not wanting to upset her further. "And they haven't accepted."

"Of course they'll come." She kicked at a pile of leaves. "It'll be the cat's meow to see Norman again. His life turned out so much more exciting than mine, stuck in boring old Timber Coulee."

I bit back a retort. Molly was far from stuck—she'd chosen to be here. "You ought to telephone Clarence and invite him to supper tonight. He and your mother should get reacquainted before the wedding."

Molly's lack of response spoke volumes. Or maybe it didn't.

Either way, I didn't like it.

As we turned onto Main Street, Callan MacTavish stood beneath Mountain Melodies' awning, hunched over a wooden crate. The telltale tremor in his hands reminded me of the war that never quite left him.

"Good morning, Callan."

He smiled, relief flashing in his eyes. "'Mornin'. I've got these horns from the school. Young Dooley dented his trumpet somethin' fierce, and there's a French horn that sounds like a dyin' moose." His brogue had strengthened during his years serving in the war on behalf of his native Scotland.

"Here, let me get the door." I fished in my handbag for my keys.

"Much obliged." He shifted the crate in his arms. "Cannae manage both the crate and the lock, I fear."

The familiar scent of wood polish and brass cleaner greeted us—the music shop that had been mine for over a decade.

Moxie dashed in first, then Callan stepped through with the crate, followed by me, then by Molly, who let the door slam. The sharp crack made Callan jump so violently he nearly dropped the crate.

"Sorry!" Molly rushed to steady it. "I didn't mean to let it slam."

"No harm done," he said quickly, but his hands shook as he set the crate down. "Just caught me off guard, is all."

I hung up my coat and hat, put on my smock, and busied myself with the mail, giving him a moment to compose himself. These episodes were becoming more frequent—sudden noises sending him into states of nervous agitation.

I brought him up to speed on Kathleen's arrival.

"Quite the disruption, I ken," he sympathized. "But family's family."

"As we work," Molly interjected, "could we listen to those new Victrola records? There's some jazz that's simply the gnat's eyebrows—"

"Jazz," Callan muttered darkly. "More o' that din."

Molly's face fell. I intervened, ever the diplomat. "Music is a matter of personal taste."

Callan shook his head. "Ach, are ye deef? 'Tisn't proper music. Music should hae structure, harmony, beauty. No' this chaotic bangin' about."

"It's not chaotic!" Molly protested. "Jazz is, well, modern. It has its own patterns and rhythms—"

"Modern." He spat the word. "Everythin' has to be modern these days, eh? What was wrong wi' the way thin's were before the war?"

As the conversation veered toward dangerous territory, I placed a hand on his forearm. "The world does seem to be changing rapidly. But perhaps some changes aren't necessarily bad."

When Callan got worked up about modernization, it led to dark moods lasting days. Molly wisely stayed quiet the rest of the morning.

Toward midmorning, Rose MacTavish entered with five-year-old Emil. Her kind eyes gave her husband a quick, assessing glance.

"Good morning. I hope Callan hasn't been working you too hard."

After favoring Moxie with a pat on the head, Emil stood on tiptoe to peer over the counter. "Papa's fixing the horn. Can I help?"

Callan's demeanor softened. "Maybe later, lad."

"I came to walk you home for lunch," Rose said, though it was barely ten. "Emil's been asking for you all morning."

I recognized the gentle subterfuge. "Since things are quiet, why don't you take the afternoon off? Molly and I can handle the shop, and you could spend time with Emil."

"I dinna need coddlin'."

"Of course not," Rose soothed, "but Emil has been so looking forward to helping you. And I'm teaching a violin lesson this afternoon."

"Besides," I added, "you can return the favor by covering tomorrow when we leave early to host dinner guests." I avoided mentioning who those guests might be, not wanting to prod the serpent, as it were.

Rose caught my eye with that meaningful look between women who cared about the same troubled man—gratitude and a plea for continued patience.

The remainder of the day passed with exhausting tension. Molly telephoned Clarence, inviting him to dinner. I telephoned Kathleen.

"Of course he should come. I'm dying to meet my future son-in-law properly. We've only exchanged letters."

"I'm thinking we'll have the chops that are in the icebox."

"Don't worry about a thing. Supper will be ready when you get home."

Maybe having my take-charge sister around wouldn't be so bad, after all.

Standing in my kitchen at half-past five, watching Kathleen commandeer my stove with the confidence of someone who cooked for threshing crews, I heard Molly answering the doorbell.

"That will be Clarence," I said.

"Right on time. Shows respect." She glanced at me. "Is James coming?"

"He's on duty tonight."

"Have you two moved closer to settling down? Neither of you is getting younger."

"If I wanted advice on the subject, I'd—oh, never mind." I took the spoon from her hand. "Go say hello. I'll be right there."

"Mrs. Mulroney, thank you for having me." Clarence's voice carried from the parlor. "I brought these for you."

I emerged to see him presenting Kathleen with late-season roses, but his gaze returned to Molly. The look that passed between them—warm and steady—made my chest tighten with recognition. Was that what James and I looked like when no one was watching?

"Well, aren't these pretty." Kathleen accepted the bouquet with obvious pleasure. "Amanda, have you got something to put these in?"

I found a crystal vase and arranged the flowers on the table. Clarence navigated the parlor like a man making the right impression. He positioned himself near Molly, not quite touching, but close enough that the air between them seemed charged.

"Please, sit." Kathleen gestured to a chair. "Molly tells me you're working at the bank while teaching music?"

"I'm an assistant clerk at Timber Coulee Bank, ma'am. The music teaching is on the side—private lessons in trumpet and theory. The bank provides steady income, and teaching is more a passion. I hope to teach full time someday." He glanced at Molly, his expression soft. "Though I've learned that the real music in life comes from finding the right harmony with someone else. Everything else is just practice."

Molly's cheeks colored, and she looked down at her hands, a smile playing at her lips. Clearly I needn't have worried that Norman the Sophisticated Saxophonist might outshine Clarence in her eyes.

"Steady income—that's important." Kathleen studied him with the frankness of someone used to judging livestock. "You're a bit thin. Do you eat regular meals?"

"I sometimes forget when I'm busy at work, ma'am."

"Well, we'll fix that tonight. I've made pork chops with potatoes and carrots, and there's a chocolate icebox cake for after. You'll have seconds of everything, or I'll want to know why."

As we moved to the dining table, Clarence's hand found the small of Molly's back, guiding her to her chair. It was such a natural gesture, so quietly possessive and protective, that I wondered if he even realized he'd done it.

The conversation hit a lull as we started in on the meal Kathleen had prepared. For all her quirks, my sister was one talented cook. Molly would do well by learning from her—as would I.

"Everything's delicious, Mrs. Mulroney." Clarence valiantly kept pace with the hearty portions Kathleen dished out. "I haven't had a home-cooked meal like this in months."

This in spite of the fact that he planted his sizeable feet under our table at least once a week. But, considering he had a future mother-in-law to impress, I let it pass.

"A man needs proper food. Molly, you're paying attention to how I've seasoned the chops, aren't you? This is the kind of thing you'll need to know."

"Yes, Mother." Molly's voice was neutral, but her hand moved toward Clarence. His fingers found hers immediately, as if drawn by instinct, and they held on.

The conversation flowed more easily as the meal progressed. Kathleen regaled Clarence with farm stories, making farm work sound both impossibly difficult and deeply satisfying.

"It's hard work, but honest work." Her fond gaze fell upon Molly. "I know our girl wasn't cut out for farm life, but I'm glad she learned the value of hard work. I'm relieved she's found a good man to marry. A woman needs that security, that partnership." She smiled at Clarence. "Her father and I are both looking forward to your wedding. Is the music all planned?"

Clarence's ears reddened, but when he looked at Molly, his expression held such open affection that even Kathleen's stern features softened for a moment.

"I just want whatever makes Molly happy, ma'am."

Molly, who'd been quieter than usual, sat up straighter at his words. She squeezed his hand once more before releasing it.

"Since you've asked, Mother, I've been thinking about the music. I'd like to invite the Midnight Serpents to perform."

The silence was profound. Even the mantel clock seemed to pause.

"The... who?"

"The Midnight Serpents. They're a jazz ensemble. Very accomplished."

"Jazz?" Kathleen set down her fork with deliberate care. "You want jazz music at your wedding?"

"At the reception, yes."

"I hear they're quite good—" I ventured. Jazz might not have been my favorite musical style, but Molly was my favorite, and only, niece.

"I'm sure they're good at making noise." Kathleen's voice was firm but not harsh. "Molly, this is the most important day of your life so far. Why would you want that kind of racket?"

"It's not racket! It's beautiful music—exciting and alive—"

"It's the kind they play in speakeasies," Kathleen said bluntly. "In those illegal drinking establishments. I may live on a farm, but I know what jazz is associated with. What will people think?"

"I don't care what people think."

"Well, you should. Reputation matters. You're going to be a music teacher's wife. Clarence will have students—families who trust him."

Clarence shifted in his seat, conflicting emotions playing across his face. He seemed to be struggling for words.

"Mrs. Mulroney," he began, with a swift side glance at Molly, "I have to admit, I'm not personally fond of jazz music myself."

The hurt that flashed across Molly's face was quickly masked, but not quickly enough.

"However," he continued, his voice gaining strength, "what matters to me isn't the style of music. What matters is that Molly cares about it deeply." He fixed his earnest gaze on Kathleen. "Your daughter has exquisite taste in music. It's one of the things I admire most about her. And I've learned that when Molly believes in something this strongly, there's usually good reason for it."

Kathleen looked too startled to come up with a reply.

"I trust her judgment, ma'am," Clarence continued, "even when it takes me to unfamiliar territory. Isn't that what marriage is—two people learning to appreciate one another's worlds?"

Molly looked at him with gratitude in her eyes. She reached for his hand again.

"You really don't like jazz?" Her voice was small.

"I don't understand it," he admitted. "The rhythm feels strange to me. But I'd like to learn. If it matters to you, then it matters."

Kathleen's lips pressed into a thin line. "At least the boy's honest. That's worth something."

"You'll see for yourself," Molly said. "The whole band is coming here for dinner tomorrow night."

"We're going to invite them," I corrected. "It's not a certainty yet."

Molly turned to Clarence. "You'll come too, won't you?"

"Wherever you are, that's where I want to be." His thumb brushed across her knuckles.

Kathleen began clearing plates with decisive movements. "I still maintain that proper wedding music comes from an organ, not from whatever it is they play in gin joints. What was wrong with the pretty music you were learning at the conservatory? That was easier on the ears. Or even a folk band."

Molly threw down her napkin. "Oh, Mother, this isn't a barn dance where you can have a fiddler and a caller and someone with a harmonica."

Time to attempt diplomacy. "Perhaps we could compromise," I broke in. "Different kinds of music at different parts of the reception? Traditional for the ceremony and dinner, then something more lively for dancing?"

All three turned to look at me, as if I'd suggested we climb up on the roof to take our dessert and coffee.

"Amanda. This is a wedding reception." Kathleen oozed patient exasperation. "It should have dignity."

"But it might work," I continued. "Older guests would appreciate traditional music, younger ones something modern—"

"If the modern portion were very brief," Clarence offered.

"And properly supervised," Kathleen added. "No wild carrying on."

Molly looked from her mother to her fiancé. "So I could have the Serpents play, but only if you both dictate how and when?"

The question exposed the problem with my diplomatic solution.

Molly pushed back from the table. "I think I need some air."

She walked out to the porch, leaving us in uncomfortable silence. Through the window, I could see her slight figure under the porch light, arms wrapped around herself.

Kathleen reached for her coffee. "She's got her father's stubborn streak. Once she gets an idea, she won't let go easily."

"Perhaps she just needs time to think it through." Clarence stood. "I'll go talk to her. Thank you both for a wonderful meal."

As Kathleen and I washed dishes, we spoke little. I couldn't help thinking how easy everything had been before her arrival, and how trouble now seemed to be swirling like dust before a storm.

***

Later that night as we crawled into bed, Kathleen confided, "I don't mind telling you, Amanda. I was disappointed when Molly left the conservatory. Not because of the music—I never understood all that, to be honest. But she'd started something. A girl needs to learn to finish what she starts."

"She's twenty-two now. Much more settled."

"I can see that, and thank the Lord for it." Kathleen turned her rag-rolled head to face me. "Working in your shop has been good for her, I'll grant you that. But when she wrote to say she was engaged—well, that's when I knew she'd found her calling. Being a wife, raising a family, making a proper home—that's what matters." She paused. "I just hope she's prepared. All that time learning scales, but can she make decent bread? Manage a household budget? That's what I'm here to teach."

"She'll be a music teacher's wife, not a farmer's wife."

"A wife is a wife. Doesn't matter if her husband teaches music or farms corn. She'll still need to know how to cook and clean and mend and manage." She gave me a look that was part concern, part subtle criticism. "I mean no offense, but you've been on your own all these years. You've never had to care for a husband, run a household, raise children. I'm not sure you'd be the one to teach Molly what she needs to know."

The words stung, though she didn't mean them unkindly. She was simply stating what she saw as fact.

"Molly's been helping me run the shop very capably."

"I'm sure. You always had a good head for business. But that's different from keeping house. I've got six weeks before Homer arrives, seven weeks until the wedding, and I plan to use every bit getting Molly ready for married life. She'll thank me later."

Moxie jumped onto the bed and began kneading the covers. Kathleen raised an eyebrow. "If you ask me, cats belong in the barn, catching mice." But she didn't shoo him away.

I switched off the lamp. But it was quite a while before I fell asleep.

Chapter Four

The next afternoon, the train whistle echoed through the valley like a siren's call, drawing half the town—mostly the younger half—to the depot platform. Some students must have cut class, eager to greet the Midnight Serpents arriving mere blocks from the high school.

Molly, Clarence, and I stood near the station house, watching curious faces emerge from shops and homes. Kathleen had insisted on staying behind to prepare dinner. I was to telephone as soon as the band accepted our invitation.

"Ten people," I'd fretted that morning. "How will I seat ten people around our little table?"

Molly had waved away my concerns. "We'll make it a picnic! Everyone can eat off plates on their laps. Cozy and informal—it'll be copacetic."

"Your mother may have opinions about guests holding plates on laps," I'd warned.

"Mother will adapt. She always does."

Now, standing on the platform, my nerves still jangled. Beside me, Clarence shifted his trumpet case from one hand to the other with obvious discomfort.

"I don't understand why we need to witness this spectacle. Surely a simple introduction before the concert would suffice."

"Don't be such a stuffed shirt," Molly's teasing carried an anxious edge. "It's a momentous occasion!"

The train rounded the bend with huffing steam and squealing brakes. The collective intake of breath was palpable. As passenger car doors opened, several ordinary travelers stepped down—a businessman with a sample case, a young man carrying a book bag.

Then the musicians began to emerge.

First came a tall, husky young man with sandy hair and kind eyes, carrying a black instrument case. He looked around with obvious curiosity. Beside me, Molly gasped.

"Norman? Norman Walsh?"

The young man's face broke into a delighted grin. "Molly Mulroney! Well, I'll be hanged! What are the odds?" He strode over, setting down his case to give Molly a warm, brotherly embrace. "Look at you—more beautiful than ever! Mountain air must agree with you."

"Norman, this is my aunt, Amanda Parrish. Aunt Amanda, this is Norman Walsh from the conservatory."

"Miss Parrish, such a pleasure." Norman's handshake was firm and sincere. "If I recall, Molly told me you own a music shop."

"Indeed—right here in Timber Coulee."

"Well, I'll be hanged," he repeated. "What are the odds?"

"And this is my fiancé, Clarence Butterworth."

Norman extended his hand warmly. "Congratulations, sir. You're getting quite a treasure in Molly—best sight-reader in our class and twice as musical as any of us."

Clarence responded with a noncommittal grunt and brief handshake, clearly on guard despite Norman's friendliness.

Three more musicians approached—a stocky, cheerful man with enormous brown eyes; a dark-skinned, lanky fellow with an instrument case slung over his shoulder; and a slight young man with wire-rimmed spectacles, clutching a worn satchel.

"Let me introduce my bandmates," Norman said. "Sal Benedetti, our drummer—best rhythm man this side of Chicago." The stocky man tipped his hat with a warm smile. "And this tall drink of water is Sweet Lou Lancaster, our trombone player."

"Ladies, gentlemen," Sweet Lou drawled pleasantly. "Pleasure to make your acquaintance."

"And our piano man, Frank Dobrowski—we call him 'Fingers.'" Norman gestured to the wiry young man, who gave a shy nod, his fingers unconsciously flexing as if practicing scales.

"Is there—would it be possible to visit the theater soon? I'd like to test the piano—"

"There'll be plenty of time, Frank. Now where's our fearless leader?" Norman looked back toward the train, irritation flashing across his features.

The crowd held its collective breath. Then Joey "Snake" Serpentine emerged from the first-class car with fluid grace, as if he'd waited for the perfect moment. He was devastatingly handsome in a way that spelled trouble for respectable young women—dark hair slicked back with pomade, piercing eyes that took in everything, and a smile promising secrets and adventures. His charcoal suit was expertly tailored, probably costing more than most folks in Timber Coulee made in six months.

Beside me, Molly's sharp intake of breath was audible, and Clarence's jaw tightened.

Joey surveyed the crowd, his smile widening. While other band members collected their luggage and gear, Joey simply stood on the platform like a king surveying his domain.

"Ladies and gentlemen of Timber Coulee!" His slightly nasal, working-class accent carried with practiced projection. "The Midnight Serpents have arrived, and we're real happy to be here in your beautiful town."

Judith Hensley, the middle-aged dress shop owner, giggled like a schoolgirl. My friend Heidi Fischer stood nearby with a dazed look. The dapper Ezra Coldwell, proprietor of the Coldwell Dance Academy, hovered near the crowd's edge, his normally composed face creased with concern. For years he'd been the arbiter of proper entertainment, teaching the young people the waltz and foxtrot and organizing the respectable Fortnightly gatherings that gave our unmarried folk a chance to socialize under careful supervision. The jazz craze had already cost him students, and now here was its living embodiment, stepping off the train like some pied piper of moral corruption.

Joey approached our group. "Norm, ain't you going to introduce me to these lovely people?"

Norman's face reddened, but his voice remained pleasant. "Of course. Joey Serpentine, I'd like you to meet my old friend from the conservatory, Miss Molly Mulroney, and her aunt, Miss Amanda Parrish. And this is Mr. Clarence Butterworth, Miss Mulroney's fiancé."

"Charmed, charmed." Joey tipped his hat. His gaze lingered on Molly with obvious appreciation. "Norman, you didn't tell me you had such attractive friends."

He turned to me. "Miss Parrish." He took my gloved hand and raised it toward his lips. I withdrew it smoothly before he could complete the kiss, offering what I hoped was a polite but cool smile.

"Mr. Serpentine. Welcome to Timber Coulee. I trust your journey was comfortable?"

"Quite comfortable. Though the destination is provin' far more enchantin' than I anticipated." His attention shifted back to Molly, and my niece's cheeks bloomed pink. "Miss Mulroney—the pleasure is mine."

"Oh! I—that is—thank you, Mr. Serpentine."

"Please, call me Joey. All the most interestin' people do."

Clarence stepped forward with barely concealed irritation. "Butterworth," he said in a curt tone, offering his hand.

"Ah, the lucky man!" Joey's smile never wavered, though I caught amusement in his eyes. "You're a fortunate fella, Mr. Butterworth. I hope you appreciate what a treasure you've found."

Frank cleared his throat nervously. "Joey, about the theater piano—should I go over now and—"

"Relax, Fingers!" Joey laughed dismissively. "The piano will still be there. You worry too much—it's just eighty-eight keys and some strings. Lighten up!"

Frank's face turned crimson, and he clutched his satchel, falling silent as nearby townspeople chuckled.

Before tension could escalate, I inserted myself back into the conversation. "Mr. Serpentine, I hope you and your band will join us for dinner this evening at our home. Nothing fancy, just a simple welcome meal."

Joey's eyebrows rose with apparent surprise and pleasure. "Why, Miss Parrish, how gracious! We'd be honored to accept." He glanced at Norman with what might have been approval. "Friends of Norman's are friends of all of us."

Norman's warm smile encompassed us both. "That's very kind. After weeks of railroad dining cars and hotel restaurants, a real home-cooked meal sounds like heaven."

"Amen to that," agreed Sal, rubbing his hands together. "My mother always said restaurant food has no soul."

Sweet Lou grinned. "Very kind, Miss Parrish. We promise to be on our best behavior."

"Wonderful." My mind was already racing toward the nearest public telephone to alert Kathleen. "Our address is one-eleven east Elm, just off Main Street. Within walking distance from your hotel. Shall we say six o'clock?"

"Perfect," Joey agreed, his charm radiating. "May we bring somethin'?"

"Just your appetites."

During our conversation, equipment had been coming off the train—instrument cases, amplification devices, trunks. While Norman, Sal, Sweet Lou, and Frank supervised loading, Joey stood aside, clearly expecting others to handle such tasks.

"Careful with that case," Joey called to a depot worker, indicating an ornate trumpet case that gleamed with brass fittings and mother-of-pearl inlays. The craftsmanship was exquisite, clearly custom-made and expensive.

Norman and Sal exchanged a look suggesting this behavior was typical, while Frank anxiously supervised the music stands and sheet music boxes.

"What a beautiful case," I commented, my professional appreciation overriding my wariness.

Joey's demeanor changed, becoming almost reverent as he ran his fingers along the edge. "This baby is my bread and butter, ma'am. A musician's horn is like his soul made manifest." For a moment, the practiced charm fell away, revealing something raw and vulnerable. "Had it made special in Chicago. Cost me three months' wages, but worth every penny."

The vulnerability in his voice caught me off guard. Whatever else Joey Serpentine might be, his love for his music seemed authentic.

"Joey! Joey!" A breathless voice cut through the crowd, and I turned to see Vivian Ashford pushing through with unseemly haste. At nineteen, Vivian worked at Murray's General Store and had been saving for teachers' college—a goal I'd been encouraging. But the young woman approaching bore little resemblance to the sensible, ambitious girl I knew.

Her usually neat brown hair had been pinned into an elaborate style that didn't suit her round face, and she'd applied rouge and lip paint with an inexperienced hand. Her dress had been altered to show more ankle than was strictly proper.

Joey's smile faltered when he saw her, discomfort flashing across his features before the charm snapped back.

"Why, hello there," he said in a neutral tone. "Miss...?"

"It's me, Vivian Ashford! From Spokane! You remember—we met after your concert at the Liberty Theater? You said I had lovely eyes!"

"Ah, yeah. Of course." Joey's smile looked strained. "How... nice to see you again."

"I can't believe you're really here! When I heard the Midnight Serpents were coming, I just knew it was fate! And did I overhear you're all invited to dinner—how wonderful! I'd love to come too, if there's room."

The silence was distinctly uncomfortable. I cleared my throat.

"I'm so sorry, Vivian, but we're already at capacity. There simply isn't room for another guest."

Vivian's face fell, but she rallied. "Oh, of course. But Joey—perhaps you could call on me tomorrow? We could take a walk, or—"

Joey said nothing, his smile now wooden.

"Vivian," I interrupted kindly, "shouldn't you be getting back to the store? Mr. Murray will be wondering."

"Oh, yes, I suppose..." She looked at Joey one more time, clearly hoping for encouragement, but he'd already turned away to speak with Norman about the luggage.

As Vivian reluctantly walked away, I caught Joey's relieved expression and filed it away for future consideration.

The equipment was loaded into a hired truck bound for the Majestic Theater, and the crowd began to disperse.

"Shall we hail a cab to the Timber Coulee Hotel?" Joey shouldered a leather bag while others handled heavier luggage.

"Oh, no. It's just a block up Main Street. Mr. Cavanaugh will see you settled comfortably." I repeated the directions to my house. "One eleven Elm Street. It's not far from the hotel."

"Excellent. Well then, Miss Parrish, Miss Molly, Mr. Butterworth—we'll see you at six sharp. I can hardly wait to experience real home cookin' and some charmin' company." His gaze lingered on Molly just long enough to make Clarence's face contort. "Until this evenin'."

I excused myself to call Kathleen from the station's public telephone. When I returned, the Midnight Serpents had started walking toward the hotel. Norman hung back slightly.

"It really is wonderful to see you again," he said to Molly, his voice warm. "You look so happy here. The conservatory seems like a lifetime ago."

"It does," Molly agreed. "Though I do miss the music sometimes. I never expected you'd end up with a jazz band."

Norman's expression grew rueful. "Well, classical music doesn't exactly pay the bills these days. Jazz is where the opportunities are, even if..." He glanced toward Joey's retreating figure and didn't finish the thought. "I suppose I'd better catch up. See you later."

On our way out we passed Ezra Coldwell still standing at the edge of the now-empty platform, staring after the musicians with an unreadable expression—a man watching his livelihood evaporate before his eyes.

"Aunt Amanda." Molly slipped an arm through mine. "He's quite... charismatic, isn't he?"

"Who? Norman?" While the young man seemed pleasant enough, *charismatic* wasn't the first word that came to mind.

"No. Joey Serpentine."

"Indeed he is." But Joey's ingratiating smile filled me with growing unease. "That's exactly what worries me."

Because in my experience, men who charmed everyone they met usually had something to hide. And something about Joey Serpentine's too-perfect smile suggested that whatever secrets he carried were the kind that could destroy the peace of our little town.

As we walked home, my mind churned with a dozen details I needed to manage before six o'clock. Ten people in my modest home, Kathleen's expectations of proper hospitality, and a band of traveling musicians probably accustomed to far more sophisticated entertainment than Timber Coulee could provide.

At least Molly's confidence was infectious. Perhaps a picnic-style dinner really would be more enjoyable than formal stuffiness. I suspected I'd know the answer by the time our guests departed.

One thing was certain. This evening would be unlike any dinner party I'd ever hosted. I just hoped I'd survive it with my reputation—and my nerves—intact.

Chapter Five

By six fifteen on Friday evening, my small cottage buzzed with an energy I'd never experienced before. Ten people milling about with plates and glasses transformed my modest home into something resembling a nightclub, though Kathleen's expression suggested she found the comparison less than flattering.

"I still think we should have set up properly at the dining table," she murmured to me as I ladled beef stew into the serving bowl. "What will people think of our hospitality?"

"They'll think we're adaptable and welcoming," I replied, watching through the kitchen window as Norman and Sweet Lou settled onto the back porch steps with their plates. Happily, the Lord had blessed us with an unseasonably warm October evening, making such *al fresco* dining possible. "Look how comfortable everyone seems."

Indeed, the informal arrangement had created a surprisingly convivial atmosphere. Sal had claimed the small kitchen table where he could regale Kathleen with stories about his Italian grandmother's cooking, while Molly and Clarence had found seats at the dining table alongside Joey, who seemed to be holding court. Frank had settled cross-legged on a cushion near the parlor's coffee table, quietly eating and listening to conversations rather than participating much. Random chairs placed here and there accommodated everyone else.

I'd popped into the kitchen to refill a breadbasket when I caught sight of movement that made me stop short. Vivian Ashford stood at the sink, washing dishes with industrious efficiency, wearing one of Kathleen's aprons over her dress.

I set down the basket and sidled up to my sister.

"Kathleen," I murmured with a raised eyebrow, "I thought we'd decided there wasn't room for additional guests."

"Oh!" Kathleen looked up from the pot she was stirring. "Vivian showed up at the back door just as I was starting to serve. Poor thing practically begged to help in the kitchen—said she didn't want to impose on the party but would be so grateful to be useful." She lowered her voice. "I couldn't very well turn her away when I needed an extra pair of hands, could I?"

Vivian was studiously focused on the dishes, though her cheeks had turned pink. Of course she'd found a way to be here, to be near Joey. The girl's determination was both admirable and concerning.

"That was kind of you to help, Vivian." I kept my tone neutral. "Thank you."

"Oh, it's my pleasure, Miss Parrish." Vivian favored me with a bright smile that may have signaled victory, or merely relief that I wasn't tossing her out. "Mrs. Mulroney's been teaching me how she seasons the stew. I'm learning so much."

Kathleen beamed, clearly pleased to have an eager student. "She's been a wonderful help, Amanda. Very quick to learn."

Vivian's eagerness surely had less to do with culinary education and more to do with the handsome trumpet player holding court at my dining table. But Kathleen was right—we did need the help, and Vivian was working hard. I couldn't fault her for that, even if her motives were transparent.

James appeared at the front door just as everyone was digging in, his hat in hand, his expression apologetic. I made introductions all around, then set about filling a plate.

"I'm so sorry to be late." He accepted the plate I handed him with a grateful smile. "The new deputy needed extra time with the arrest procedures. There are some particular challenges when dealing with female prisoners."

"Female prisoners? I didn't know Timber Coulee had any." Not since a couple of years earlier, anyway, when a vivacious con artist had tried to swindle soldiers' families in a complicated fraud scheme.

"Mostly women involved in smuggling liquor. The department thought it wise to bring in a female deputy to handle searches and such—makes everyone more comfortable." James looked around at the scattered diners with obvious pleasure. "This looks wonderful, Amanda. Much more relaxed than a formal dinner."

"A female deputy." A silent-screen stereotype of a prison matron in a severe uniform, with iron-gray hair, arms like ham hocks, and a face etched in deep frown lines came to mind. "She must be quite capable to handle such difficult work."

"Deputy Marshal Margaret O'Brien. She's extremely professional." James turned his attention to Sweet Lou, who was refilling his plate at the buffet. "Excuse me, sir. I have to admit, I'm fascinated by your music. Is it true that jazz musicians make it up as they go along?"

His interest surprised me—James had never mentioned any curiosity about jazz before. But then again, we'd always discussed other types of music when the topic came up, which wasn't often. Acknowledging my love for certain classical composers, he'd told me once that he was more of a gospel-music man himself.

Sweet Lou shrugged. "Ain't exactly makin' it up, Sheriff. There's structure and technique involved, but a lotta room for improvisation, too."

Frank looked up from his cushion. "The piano provides the harmonic foundation, so I have to be ready to follow wherever the others lead. It's... it's actually quite challenging."

"Like havin' a conversation," Joey added from the dining table, gesturing with his fork. "You know the language, but you choose your words in the moment to express what you're feelin'."

"Fascinating." James's interest was genuine. "I'd love to hear more about the technical aspects."

Just then, Moxie made his grand entrance, padding into the parlor with the regal bearing of a cat who knew he belonged wherever he chose to be. He made his usual rounds, weaving between chair legs and investigating shoes with aristocratic disdain, accepting the occasional scratch behind the ears from those who knew how to properly honor a feline.

But when he reached Sal at the kitchen table, something changed.

The cat stopped dead, his whiskers twitching. Then, to my complete astonishment, he rubbed against Sal's leg with unusual enthusiasm, purring loudly enough that I could hear it from across the room.

"Well, hello there, little fella." Sal looked down with obvious discomfort. He shifted his leg away slightly, but Moxie persisted, now attempting to climb into his lap.

"Moxie, no," I called. "I'm so sorry—he's usually a little more standoffish with strangers."

"It's all right." Sal's expression suggested otherwise. He gently but firmly set Moxie back on the floor. "I ain't much of a cat person, to be honest. Had a bad experience with one as a kid."

But Moxie seemed utterly smitten. He wound around Sal's ankles in figure-eights, his tail held high, continuing his loud, rattling purr.

Kathleen laughed from the stove. "Well, I've never seen him take to anyone like that! You must have a way with animals, Mr. Benedetti, whether you know it or not."

Sal looked uncertain, reaching down to move Moxie away once more as the cat tried to climb his leg. "If you say so, ma'am. Though I think he's got me confused with somebody else."

"Moxie, come here." I scooped up the cat and carried him to the kitchen door, where I shooed him out onto the back porch. "Go outside and keep Norman company."

I apologized to Sal again, then returned to my other guests. As the evening progressed, I moved among the various groups, refilling glasses and absorbing the conversations that swirled around my home like musical counterpoint. For all my worrying, everyone seemed to be having a wonderful time, and I was grateful to Molly for suggesting it in the first place.

Later, while passing the dining table, I caught the tail end of what seemed to be a heated discussion between Clarence and Joey.

"—proper embouchure is essential," Clarence was saying, his voice tight with controlled irritation. "Without correct mouth position, the tone suffers terribly."

"Oh, absolutely," Joey agreed. "Though I've found that rigid adherence to classical technique can sometimes limit one's expression. Jazz requires a more... flexible approach."

Clarence's face reddened slightly. "Flexibility is one thing, but abandoning fundamental principles entirely—"

"Now, now, gentlemen." Molly laughed. "You're both excellent musicians. Surely there's room for different styles?"

But by the tension in Clarence's shoulders, the way his jaw tightened when Joey leaned toward Molly as he spoke—this wasn't really about trumpet technique at all.

Moving to the kitchen, I found Sal regaling Kathleen with tales of the band's travels while she fussed over whether he'd eaten enough. Vivian hovered nearby, ostensibly washing dishes but clearly listening to every word.

"You boys are too thin," Kathleen said, attempting to add another spoonful of stew to his plate—amusing since Sal's physique suggested he never missed a meal. But this was the motherly side of Kathleen taking over. "All this traveling and restaurant food—it's not healthy for young men."

"You sound just like my nonna." Sal laughed. "She always said the same thing. But you know, Mrs. Mulroney, it gets tiring after a while, all this moving from town to town."

Kathleen's expression softened with maternal concern. "I imagine it would. Don't you ever want to settle down somewhere?"

"Every day," Sal admitted. "Problem is, Joey's got the star power that draws the crowds. Without him..." He shrugged philosophically. "Poor Frank out there jumps every time Joey looks at him sideways. We all know who calls the shots."

After dinner, as the men drifted toward the front porch for some fresh air, Sal patted his jacket pocket and pulled out a worn leather tobacco pouch and a small briar pipe.

"Mrs. Mulroney, would you mind terribly if I stepped outside for a smoke?" he asked politely. "I know some ladies don't care for it indoors."

"Oh, not at all," Kathleen said. "That's very considerate of you. The porch should be comfortable—it's still quite mild out."

No sooner had he opened the door than Moxie suddenly appeared from nowhere, weaving between his feet with renewed enthusiasm, nearly tripping him.

"Moxie!" I grabbed the cat again, bewildered by his behavior. "What has gotten into you tonight?"

Sal chuckled as he escaped to the porch. "Wish the ladies showed as much interest in me as that cat does."

Norman and Sweet Lou joined him outside. The glow of Sal's pipe as he lit it came through the window, the sweet-smelling smoke drifting in through the open door.

I carried my recalcitrant feline through the house and incarcerated him in my bedroom.

Later, after Sal had come back inside and was helping himself to another bowl of stew, I stepped onto the porch to check on Norman and Sweet Lou. Their conversation made me pause just inside the doorway.

"—getting harder to work with." Norman's usually cheerful voice was subdued. "Did you see how he just stood there at the station while we loaded everything? Like he's too good to handle his own equipment."

Sweet Lou 's nod was grim. "And the way he talks to Sal sometimes. We're supposed to be equal partners in this band, but Joey acts like the big cheese, like he's doin' us a favor lettin' us play with him. You shoulda seen how he shut down Fingers's question about the piano."

"Maybe I should talk to him," Norman suggested. "We've been friends longer than the others. He might listen to me."

"If he don't listen to Sal, who's blood, what makes you think he'll listen to you?"

"I don't know, but it might be worth a shot."

"Good luck with that." Sweet Lou noticed me in the doorway. "Oh, Miss Parrish! Sorry, we didn't mean to—"

"No need to apologize." I stepped fully onto the porch. "I was just checking if you needed anything. More coffee, perhaps?"

The moment passed, but I filed away their concerns about Joey's behavior. In a small group like a traveling band, personality conflicts could become quite serious.

Norman stood. "No thank you. The meal was delicious. But it's getting chilly out here. What do you say we go inside?"

Back in the parlor, we found James in conversation with Joey and several others near the front window.

"—you know, I have to say, Timber Coulee has really impressed me. The turnout at the station today, all these enthusiastic young faces—there's clearly an appetite for modern entertainment here."

"You think so?" James asked with interest.

"Oh, yeah. I been thinkin'—and this is just a thought, mind you—but a fella could do well openin' a proper jazz establishment in a town like this. Somewhere the kids could come to hear real music, maybe dance a little." Joey's eyes took on a dreamy quality. "I'm gettin' tired of life on the road, to tell you the truth. All these hotels and train schedules—a man starts to crave puttin' down roots somewhere."

Sal's head turned sharply from across the room, his expression troubled, while Frank looked up from his cushion with obvious alarm.

"You talkin' permanently?" Sweet Lou's voice carried a note of concern.

"Just thinkin' out loud." Joey gave them a casual wave. "I ain't abandonin' you boys mid-tour or anythin'. But a fella's gotta think about the future, right? Can't be travelin' forever."

The silence that followed was heavy with unspoken implications. I could practically see the calculations running through the other band members' minds—their livelihood depended on Joey's star power, and they all knew it.

Molly's laughter from the kitchen broke the tension, and I turned to see Norman entertaining her and Clarence with what appeared to be an animated story.

"—so there I am, trying to concentrate on this incredibly difficult piece for my final exam." He gestured wildly. "And I'm so focused on the sight-reading that I don't notice my music stand is slowly sliding down, bit by bit."

Molly gasped. "Oh, Norman, you didn't!"

"I kept adjusting my posture to follow the music lower and lower, until I was practically bent in half! Still playing perfectly, mind you, but looking like some sort of musical contortionist. The professor and half the class were trying not to laugh, and I had no idea why until I finished the piece and stood up straight again."

Even Clarence was chuckling at the image. Thank goodness, some of the tension had left his face, and Molly wiped tears of laughter from her eyes.

Back in the parlor, the conversation had turned to various musical mishaps when someone—Sweet Lou, maybe—made a comment that caught my attention.

"At least you ain't got some Stage-Door Sally traipsin' after you like Joey does in every town."

Joey gave a dismissive wave. "Oh, that's just part of the business. Ladies get excited about the music, that's all."

"Like that girl today at the station?" Norman added with a knowing look. "What was her name—Victoria? Virginia?"

I glanced quickly toward the kitchen doorway, hoping Vivian hadn't overheard this conversation. I couldn't see her from where I stood, but I kept my voice low as I corrected them.

"Vivian," I hissed. "Her name is Vivian Ashford, and she's a perfectly respectable girl who works at the general store while she saves money for college."

Joey looked blank for a moment. "Oh, right. The one from… where was it? Spokane?"

His casual dismissal made my jaw tighten. "She obviously remembers you quite well."

"Nice girl, I'm sure," Joey said with practiced charm, clearly not remembering Vivian at all. "I meet so many people on tour, sometimes the faces blur together."

"That's the problem with you musician types," James teased. "A girl in every port, like sailors."

The other men laughed, but I found nothing amusing about Vivian's obvious infatuation being treated so lightly. The poor girl had probably been counting the days until the band's arrival, while Joey hadn't given her a second thought.

As the evening wound down and people dispersed throughout the house again, James helped Kathleen clear plates with easy efficiency. My sister seemed quite taken with his polite manners and willingness to help.

"Such a gentleman," she murmured to me with approval. "And he seems genuinely interested in getting to know everyone. That shows good character."

It was true—James had spent time talking with each of the band members, asking thoughtful questions about their music and travels. His nature made him a good listener, and several of the men had warmed to him considerably.

"Thank you for including me tonight," he whispered as he carried a stack of plates to the kitchen. "I know you were already managing quite a crowd."

"You're always welcome at my table." I meant it completely. "Though I have to admit, I'm curious about this interest in jazz music. You've never mentioned it before."

He looked slightly embarrassed. "I suppose I assumed you'd disapprove, given your classical training. But I've always been fascinated by the... spontaneity of it. The way musicians can communicate with each other in the moment."

"I don't disapprove of anything that brings people joy," I said, surprised to realize I meant it. "Though I admit, I'm still learning to appreciate it myself."

Just as I was beginning to think the evening had passed without major incident, Kathleen emerged from the kitchen carrying a magnificent apple torte, its golden crust gleaming with sugar crystals. Vivian followed behind her, carrying smaller dessert plates.

"I hope everyone saved room for dessert," Kathleen announced with obvious pride. "This is an old family recipe—my grandmother's apple torte with cinnamon, nutmeg, and anise. Amanda, could you bring me a cake server?"

I opened a drawer in the sideboard, pulled out a silver serving utensil, and set it on the table. The appreciative murmurs elicited by Kathleen's masterpiece suddenly stopped when Joey raised his hand with a look of distress.

"Oh, I'm terribly sorry, Mrs. Mulroney, but I can't have anything with anise. It gives me the most dreadful reaction—my throat closes up, and I break out in a rash. Nearly killed me once when I was a kid."

Behind Kathleen, Vivian's eyes widened with alarm, her hand flying to her mouth. She'd been standing close enough to hear every word.

Kathleen's face fell with disappointment. "Oh my! I had no idea—"

"Don't you worry about it." Joey's charm worked to smooth over her embarrassment. "It's been a problem my whole life. You can imagine how inconvenient it was, growin' up in an Italian household where anise goes into everything from cookies to Sunday gravy."

Sal looked up from his plate with a knowing nod. "He ain't kiddin'. Our nonna used to say anise was God's gift to the kitchen. Every feast day, every celebration—anise in the bread, anise in the wine, anise everywhere you looked."

"Exactly!" Joey grinned and slapped his knee.

"Wait a minute," I said. "You two have the same grandmother? You're brothers?"

"Cousins. Our moms were sisters. Grew up together in Chicago's Little Italy. He ain't jokin' about the anise." Sal stabbed his fork in the air for emphasis. "At my ninth birthday party, he ended up in the hospital."

"Storebought cake instead of homemade." Joey winked at Kathleen, who'd understand the difference.

"My mother still feels bad about it," Sal said.

"She don't need to feel bad." Joey clapped Sal on the back. "I'm still here, ain't I?"

"Yeah, you are."

Vivian gazed at Joey, the dessert plates trembling slightly in her hands, silently begging him to notice her. But everyone's focus was on Joey and the dramatic revelation about his allergy.

"Well, I feel terrible about this." Kathleen held the torte as if uncertain what to do with it. "I wish I'd known—I may have some chocolate icebox cake left over, but—"

"Mrs. Mulroney, please don't give it another thought," Joey assured her. "Besides, I've been so busy enjoyin' that incredible beef stew, I'm not sure I have room for dessert anyway. What was your secret? I've never tasted anythin' quite like it."

Kathleen glowed under his praise. "Oh, it's nothing special—just a bit of thyme and bay leaves, and I always add a splash of red wine to the broth."

"Well, it was absolutely magnificent," Joey declared. "The best home cookin' I've had in months. You're a treasure, Mrs. Mulroney."

My sister's cheeks turned pink with pleasure as she warmed to Joey's extravagant compliments.

"Perhaps I could make you something special tomorrow," she offered eagerly. "Something you can eat."

"That would be incredibly kind of you," Joey replied. "Though you've already done so much."

Sal chuckled. "You'd better say yes, Joey. When a lady wants to feed you, you don't argue."

"Got that right." Joey grinned. "Our own nonna would have boxed my ears for refusin' a lady's cookin'."

It was unclear whether Kathleen heard the last few remarks, because she was examining the silver serving utensil with a frown. She emitted a longsuffering sigh, gave the slicer a quick swipe with a corner of her apron, then set to dividing up the cake.

When everyone had finished dessert, Vivian came to clear the plates.

Sal shot to his feet. "Here, let me help you with that. " He took some of the plates from her, then followed her to the kitchen.

"Thank you," Vivian said, her voice soft and hesitant. From my position near the kitchen doorway I heard her add, "That was awful, what Joey went through as a child. It must have been so frightening."

Sal's response was equally quiet, but there was warmth in it. "Yeah, it was pretty scary. But Joey's tough—always has been." He paused, then added: "You're a good person, you know that? Not many people would've worked as hard as you did tonight just to help out."

"Oh, I was happy to help Mrs. Mulroney," Vivian assured him.

"I'm sure you were." Something in Sal's tone made me glance toward the kitchen again. He was looking at Vivian with an expression I couldn't quite read—kindness mixed with something that might have been sympathy, or perhaps recognition. "A pretty girl like you shouldn't have to work so hard."

Vivian murmured something I couldn't hear, and then Sal returned to the parlor with his coffee cup, passing me with a friendly nod.

I filed the moment away without much thought. Sal was being kind to Vivian, that was all. The poor girl had worked hard all evening, and his small compliment had probably meant a great deal to her, especially after the way Joey had dismissed her earlier.

As the evening drew to a close, I reflected on the various currents that had flowed through my small cottage that night. The casual bonhomie on the surface, the tensions simmering underneath—Joey's casual arrogance, Norman's growing frustration, Clarence's jealousy, the other band members' concerns about their future, Frank's obvious nervousness around Joey. Even Kathleen had seemed to soften toward the musicians by evening's end, though she still clucked disapprovingly when Sweet Lou lit up a cigarette on the front porch.

"They're good boys. A bit rough around the edges, perhaps, but good-hearted," Kathleen said to me as we closed the door behind the last Midnight Serpent. Vivian had slipped away earlier, thanking Kathleen profusely for letting her help, and Clarence and Molly sat together in the shadows of the porch.

I nodded, though I wasn't entirely sure I shared my sister's assessment of all of them. Joey Serpentine remained an enigma—charming and talented, certainly, but with an ego that seemed to grow larger with every compliment and a casual disregard for the feelings of others that troubled me.

As James lingered to help with the last of the cleanup, I hoped the band's brief stay in Timber Coulee would pass without incident. But something about the evening's tensions made me suspect that harmony might be harder to maintain than anyone anticipated.

Chapter Six

I was pinning up my hair in front of my bedroom mirror Saturday morning when Kathleen appeared in the doorway, already fully dressed despite the early hour. Her expression held that particular determination I'd learned to recognize—and dread.

"Amanda, I forgot to mention it when we were cleaning up last night, but your silver is a disgrace."

My hand froze mid-pin. "I'm sorry, what?"

"That silver cake slicer. It was tarnished. Tarnished! What would Grandma Parrish say?"

"She'd probably say she was just glad it was getting some use," I retorted. "I don't have many occasions to bring it out."

"Why she bothered leaving it all to you, I'll never know."

"Because you received all of Grandma Mulroney's. Fair's fair."

She ignored that. "You need to give me all the silver. The serving pieces, flatware, anything that might be tarnished." She stepped into the room, her gaze sweeping across my modest dresser as if silver services might be hiding among my hairbrushes and cologne bottles. "I need to teach Molly proper care of silver before her wedding."

"Kathleen, it's Saturday. We're opening the shop for a half day, and then we need time to prepare for the concert tonight."

"Which gives us the entire morning." Kathleen was unmoved. "Won't take more than a few hours. Surely you can do without her at the store. You have Callan. Do you have the rest of the silver or not?"

I met my sister's eyes in the mirror. "All of Grandma Parrish's serving pieces are in the dining room hutch."

"Perfect. Get them out, please. I'll collect Molly." She was already turning toward the hallway.

"Kathleen, wait—" But she was gone, her footsteps brisk and purposeful as she headed for Molly's small room.

I rushed to finish pinning my hair, then descended to the dining room where I retrieved the serving dishes and a wooden box of silverware from the hutch. Through the ceiling, Molly's voice rose in protest, followed by Kathleen's firm, measured responses.

A few minutes later, Molly appeared on the stairs, still in her dressing gown, her hair loose around her shoulders. The excitement that had lit her face the previous night had been replaced by mutinous resignation.

"Mother says I can't get dressed until after the silver lesson," she announced, her voice tight with frustration. "Because I might get polish on my good clothes."

"That's sensible." I tried for diplomacy.

"That's ridiculous. The concert is tonight. Tonight! And instead of thinking about music and dancing and Clarence and seeing Norman play, I'm going to spend my morning polishing spoons." She dropped into a dining room chair with rather more force than necessary.

Kathleen descended the stairs carrying her carpetbag, from which she produced a jar of silver polish and several soft cloths. "A bride must know how to care for her household treasures. Molly, come to the kitchen. The light is better there, and we don't want to damage Amanda's dining table."

I followed them, carrying the box of tarnished silver, and set it on the kitchen table. Kathleen unwrapped the pieces one by one—creamer, sugar bowl, serving spoons, butter knife, small tray. In the morning light streaming through the windows, the tarnish was even more apparent than I'd remembered, a dark fog obscuring what had once been brilliant shine.

"Oh, my." Kathleen's voice held true distress. "Amanda, when was the last time you polished these?"

"Two years ago? Perhaps three?" A small current of shame ran under my indignation. Did tarnish mark me a failure as a woman? "I don't often use them."

"These were Grandma Parrish's wedding pieces." Kathleen lifted the creamer with almost reverent care. "They deserve better."

Molly picked up one of the serving spoons, her nose wrinkling at the blackened surface. "It looks diseased."

"That's tarnish. Silver reacts with sulfur compounds in the air." Kathleen set the creamer back down and arranged the polish and cloths. "Now, watch carefully. You never scrub in circles—that can leave scratches. Long, smooth strokes, following the grain of the metal."

She demonstrated on the sugar bowl, her movements practiced and sure. Where the cloth passed, the dark coating lifted away, revealing gleaming silver beneath.

"See? It's not difficult, but it requires patience and attention to detail. These are the qualities that separate the adequate from the excellent in all things—homemaking, music, life itself."

I checked the kitchen clock. Nearly seven-thirty. "I need to open the shop at eight. Callan's expecting me."

"Go ahead." Kathleen dismissed me without looking up. "We'll be fine here."

Molly's eyes pleaded with me not to abandon her, but I had little choice. "We close at noon on Saturdays," I reminded her. "You'll still have plenty of time this afternoon to prepare for the concert. I promise."

"If Mother doesn't invent another 'essential' lesson," Molly muttered, but she took the cloth and polish that Kathleen handed her and began working on the creamer with visible reluctance.

I escaped upstairs to finish dressing, then gathered my things for work. When I came back down, they were seated side by side at the table, their heads bent over the silver, Kathleen's hands guiding Molly's.

"Gentler pressure," Kathleen was saying. "Let the polish do the work. Steady rhythm, like this."

I slipped out the front door, leaving them to their domestic tutorial. But as I walked toward Mountain Melodies in the crisp autumn air, the scene I'd left behind followed me. Molly's frustration was obvious, yes. But there had been something else too—the way she'd adjusted her grip when Kathleen corrected her, the small nod of satisfaction when the creamer began to emerge from its tarnished cocoon.

The morning at Mountain Melodies passed quietly. Callan arrived shortly after I did, and we worked companionably on instrument repairs and customer inquiries. A few people came in asking about the concert that evening—apparently word had spread throughout town about the Midnight Serpents' arrival. I sold several jazz records to customers who wanted to "understand what all the fuss was about," as one older gentleman put it.

Around eleven-thirty, just as I was preparing to close for the afternoon, the shop door opened and Molly entered with Kathleen. Molly's hair was now properly pinned, and she wore her second-best day dress—the brown one with cream trim. Both women looked tired.

"Six pieces of silver," Molly announced before I even said hello. "It took us nearly four hours to polish six pieces of silver. Mother made me redo the creamer twice because she claimed I'd left tarnish in the crevices. I couldn't even see it."

"I could see the shadow of it," Kathleen said mildly. "Your future in-laws will notice such details, even if you don't."

"Clarence's family lives in Montana. They're not going to inspect my silver with a magnifying glass."

"Attention to detail separates the adequate from the excellent," Kathleen replied. "You'll thank me someday when you're entertaining Clarence's students' families and they comment on how beautifully your table is set."

"If I'm entertaining Clarence's students' families, I'll be too worried about the food to care about the silver," Molly retorted, but there was less heat in her voice than there might have been.

I noticed something else too—when Molly held out her hands to show me the polish residue still faintly visible on her fingers, they were steady and capable. And despite her complaints, there was a small, almost secretive smile playing at the corners of her mouth.

"Well." I locked the shop door behind us. "You still have the whole afternoon before we need to leave for the theater. Plenty of time to rest and get ready. We want to look our best."

"Thank heaven," Molly said. "Though Mother will probably insist I practice my needlework or learn to render lard or something equally thrilling."

"I was actually thinking you could take a nap," Kathleen said. "You were up half the night playing that infernal jazz music on the gramophone. A bride needs proper rest."

Molly looked so surprised by this concession that she stopped walking. "Really?"

"Really. You did well this morning. Better than I expected, truth be told." Kathleen's expression softened just slightly. "Your great-grandmother would have been pleased to see you care for her things with such attention."

As we walked home together, I caught Molly touching her fingertips together, no doubt feeling the slight roughness left by the polishing compound. And when Kathleen wasn't looking, she glanced at her mother with an expression I couldn't quite read—somewhere between annoyance and affection, between resistance and reluctant respect.

Perhaps Kathleen's lessons were having more effect than any of us wanted to admit.

***

On Saturday evening, the sidewalk outside the Majestic Theater buzzed with an energy I hadn't seen in our sleepy little town since the Fourth of July. Main Street thronged with townspeople heading toward the theater, their chatter filling the October evening air. Groups of young people clustered near the entrance, their animated conversations punctuated by nervous laughter, while their elders approached with the cautious dignity of soldiers entering potentially hostile territory.

I smoothed my navy wool dress and adjusted my hat, grateful I'd chosen something that struck a balance between respectability and style. James offered his arm as we approached the theater, and I sensed the familiar comfort of his solid presence beside me.

"Quite a turnout." His keen eyes scanned the crowd with professional interest. "I haven't seen this many people gathered in one place since the harvest festival."

"Half of them probably came hoping to be scandalized." I nodded toward Reverend Miller's conspicuous position near the front entrance, notebook already in hand. "And the other half hoping to scandalize someone else."

James chuckled, pressing my arm beneath his as we navigated through the crowd. "Well, at least if there's any trouble, I'll have plenty of witnesses."

We'd been keeping company for over a year now—long enough that his protective gestures felt natural rather than presumptuous, though not so long that the tongues had stopped wagging entirely. James was a good man, steady and kind, with laugh lines around his brown eyes that deepened when he smiled. His late wife, Sara, had been my good friend, and I'd always liked and admired him. But following Sara's death, something about our easy friendship had gradually—and with some hesitation—blossomed into romance.

"James! There you are." A confident feminine voice cut through the crowd. An attractive woman in her late twenties approached us with a brisk, purposeful stride. She wore a lovely aquamarine dress that made her blue eyes stand out. I gave myself an inward kick for not wearing my own blue dress... the one James liked so much.

"Amanda, I'd like you to meet Deputy Margaret O'Brien." James's voice carried a note of pride. "Deputy, this is Amanda Parrish, the woman I've been telling you about."

"Miss Parrish." The deputy extended a firm handshake, her eyes bright with intelligence. "Sheriff Holcomb speaks of you constantly. It's wonderful to meet the woman who's captured our sheriff's attention."

Her smile was genuine and warm, her manner friendly and professional, and I should have liked her immediately. Instead, a sharp, unexpected stab of something that took me a moment to identify as jealousy—both romantic and professional in nature—hit me.

Unlike the gray-haired, matronly deputy of my imagination, Margaret O'Brien was undeniably beautiful, with blonde hair neatly pinned beneath her hat and the kind of self-assured bearing that came from a woman accustomed to being admired. But it was more than her attractiveness that unsettled me. It was the easy way she and James stood together, the obvious familiarity in their professional rapport, the way they shared a world of law enforcement that I could never fully understand or participate in, much as I might have liked to.

"Deputy O'Brien is new to our district," James explained. "She transferred here from Boise. Already proving invaluable—her investigative skills are exceptional."

"Pleased to meet you, Deputy O'Brien." My smile, even my voice, felt stiff and unnatural. What in the world was wrong with me?

"I'm glad to meet you too." She seemed oblivious to my internal turmoil. "Sheriff Holcomb tells me you own the music shop on Main Street. What an interesting profession for a woman. You must have quite a head for business."

"I manage well enough." I willed my lips to remain smiling. "Have you had much experience with criminal investigations, Deputy?"

"Some. I worked on several fraud cases in Boise, and I helped solve a robbery ring that had been plaguing the city for months." Her eyes lit up with obvious enthusiasm for her work. "There's something deeply satisfying about putting together the pieces of a puzzle until the truth emerges."

James nodded in approval. "Deputy O'Brien has a real talent for seeing patterns others miss. Just yesterday, she identified a connection between two seemingly unrelated thefts that had us stumped."

Their professional intimacy stung more than I cared to admit. I'd always prided myself on being an independent woman who didn't need validation from a man, but watching James's obvious respect for Deputy O'Brien's abilities made me acutely aware of how little I truly knew about the work that defined so much of his life.

"How fascinating," I managed, grateful when the theater doors opened and the crowd shuffled forward.

The Majestic's interior gleamed under the electric lights, its red velvet seats and gilded details creating an atmosphere of sophisticated entertainment that seemed almost foreign to our mountain town. As we found our seats—James had secured excellent spots in the fourth row, albeit for Deputy O'Brien as well as ourselves—I recognized faces throughout the audience.

Molly sat with Clarence and Kathleen in the row in front of us, my niece vibrating with excitement while her fiancé maintained the resigned expression of a man attending his own execution. Rose MacTavish had claimed seats near the back with several other wives, while their husbands clustered in a group that included Dr. Moriarty and banker Michael Tate and his wife, Carrie, director of the summer music camp. Callan was absent, which didn't surprise me, given his dislike of loud noises in general, and jazz in particular. He and Emil were no doubt enjoying a fun-filled father-and-son evening at home.

Ezra Coldwell sat alone near the side aisle, his usually proud appearance somehow diminished as he watched his regular students chattering excitedly about the evening's entertainment. Poor Ezra looked like a man watching his life's work crumble before his eyes.

But it was Vivian Ashford who caught my attention most. She and her friends had managed to secure a seat in the very front row, directly in front of where the band would perform, and her appearance had undergone another transformation since the previous afternoon. Her dress was cut lower than anything I'd seen her wear before, her hair was elaborately styled with fashionable finger waves, and she'd applied cosmetics with a heavier hand than any respectable working girl should dare.

"That young woman looks like she's dressed for a different sort of entertainment entirely," Deputy O'Brien observed, following my gaze.

"Vivian works at Murray's General Store," I whispered. "She's been saving money for teachers' college, or at least she was until recently. She's an avid admirer of the bandleader."

"Ah." The deputy's tone suggested she understood the implications. "The sort of girl who might be easily impressed by a handsome musician wearing expensive clothes and spouting smooth words."

Her assessment was uncomfortably accurate, and I grudgingly appreciated her perceptiveness even as it irritated me.

The lights dimmed, and the Midnight Serpents took the stage to enthusiastic applause from the younger portion of the audience. Joey emerged last, resplendent in a black tuxedo that fit him like a second skin, his ornate trumpet case glinting under the stage lights as he set it carefully on a small table.

"Ladies and gentlemen of Timber Coulee." His voice carried easily to the back of the theater. "Tonight we're gonna take you on a musical journey unlike anything you've ever experienced. We're gonna show you what happens when music breaks free from the dusty confines of tradition and reaches for somethin' wild, somethin' alive, somethin' that speaks directly to the human heart."

Reverend Miller's pencil raced frantically across his notebook.

Joey opened his trumpet case with theatrical flair, revealing an instrument that gleamed like molten gold under the lights. Even from our seats, I could see it was a work of art—not just a musical instrument but a masterpiece of craftsmanship that probably cost more than most people in the audience earned in a year.

The first notes that emerged from Joey's trumpet silenced every conversation in the theater. His tone was pure liquid silk, weaving a melody so hauntingly beautiful that even the most determined skeptics leaned forward despite themselves. The other musicians joined in gradually—piano, drums, saxophone—building a complex musical landscape that was both alien and irresistibly compelling.

This wasn't the chaotic noise that jazz's detractors claimed it to be. This was sophisticated, masterful music performed by gifted artists who understood their craft completely. Joey's improvisation was nothing short of brilliant, taking melodic lines I recognized from popular songs and transforming them into something entirely new and magical.

I tapped my foot despite my reservations, and when I glanced around the theater, I saw similar capitulation everywhere. Judith Hensley swayed in her seat. Dr. Moriarty bobbed his head along with the rhythm. Even Clarence had stopped scowling, his head cocked with obvious professional interest.

The younger members of the audience were completely enthralled. Several couples danced in the aisles, their movements fluid and modern in a way that would have been scandalous just a few years earlier. Molly watched the dancers with obvious longing, though Clarence's disapproving presence kept her firmly in her seat. "It's a concert, not a free-for-all," he stage-whispered in her ear.

During a particularly energetic number, James watched the crowd with professional interest rather than enjoying the music. "Everything all right?" I murmured.

"Just keeping an eye on things," he replied. "This level of excitement can sometimes lead to poor judgment."

Deputy O'Brien leaned over from James's other side. "The crowd dynamics are fascinating," she said. "Look how the generational lines are being drawn. The younger folks are embracing this completely, while their elders are struggling between attraction and moral objection."

Her analytical observation was astute. She could read social undercurrents while still enjoying the performance. No wonder James valued her skills.

When intermission arrived, the theater buzzed with animated conversation. Some audience members headed for the lobby, while others remained in their seats, discussing what they'd just witnessed. Molly leaned over the row of seats and asked me, "Where do you think I might find Norman?"

"Look backstage, in the green room."

She nodded and headed down the aisle. James leaned toward me and muttered, "What's a green room?"

"It's a private room backstage where performers go to rest and prepare," I replied. "Most theaters have one."

"Is it always green?"

"No."

"Then why do they call it a green room?"

"I don't know. It's just one of those kooky theater traditions, I suppose, like telling someone to 'break a leg' instead of wishing them good luck, or not saying 'MacBeth' out loud in a theater. You're supposed to say 'the Scottish play' instead."

"But why?" Deputy O'Brien asked.

"Just silly superstitions." Feeling ill-equipped to expound on all legends theatrical, I was about to suggest we step outside for fresh air when a commotion near the stage caught my attention.

Clarence had approached the musicians, his own trumpet case in hand, and was speaking earnestly with Joey. Their conversation grew animated, and Joey's trademark smile took on a sharper edge.

"I think your young friend may be about to make a mistake," Deputy O'Brien observed quietly.

She was right. Clarence was clearly challenging Joey to some sort of musical competition, his classical training making him confident in his abilities. What he didn't seem to understand was that he was entering a completely different arena than the one he'd been trained for.

"Ah, a cuttin' contest!" Joey announced loudly enough for most of the theater to hear. "Ladies and gentlemen, Mr. Butterworth here has graciously offered to engage in a friendly musical duel. Shall we give it a go?"

The crowd pressed closer to the stage, sensing drama. Molly stopped in her tracks on her way backstage, while Kathleen appeared torn between pride in her future son-in-law's musical abilities and horror at such a public display.

Clarence went first, playing a technically perfect rendition of a Bach trumpet voluntary. His tone was pure, his technique flawless, his interpretation respectful of the composer's intentions. It was everything a classically trained musician should be—precise, beautiful, and completely predictable.

The applause was polite and appreciative.

Then Joey stepped forward with that dangerous smile, raised his golden trumpet, and proceeded to demolish everything Clarence had just accomplished. He began with the same Bach melody but immediately deconstructed it, twisting the familiar phrases into something wild and unexpected. His improvisation was fearless, taking risks that would have terrified a classically trained musician, and somehow making every daring choice work perfectly.

The audience went wild. Even those who had come prepared to disapprove were caught up in the sheer audacity and skill of his performance. When he finally lowered his trumpet, the theater erupted in thunderous applause.

Clarence stood frozen, his face pale with humiliation. The contrast between his safe, scholarly performance and Joey's electrifying artistry couldn't have been more stark.

Joey approached him with that predatory smile, speaking loudly enough for everyone to hear: "Not bad for classical trainin', pal. Though I find that kind of rigid instruction makes a man soft. The world's changin', and music's gotta change with it."

Clarence flinched as if the words were physical blows. Molly's face flushed with indignation on her fiancé's behalf, while Kathleen's expression suggested she might be reassessing her future son-in-law's worthiness. Clarence retreated to his seat in mortified silence, the life gone out of him like air from a punctured balloon.

"That was unnecessarily cruel," I murmured to James.

"Indeed." His jaw tightened with disapproval. "There's a difference between winning gracefully and humiliating your opponent."

Joey sauntered into the audience, accepting congratulations and back-slaps with practiced ease. But as he passed our seats, I caught something in his eyes—not triumph, but a flicker of something darker. Fear, perhaps, or calculation. The kind of look a cornered animal wears just before it bites.

Molly abandoned her quest to find Norman and instead snuggled beside her fiancé, touching his arm and speaking earnest words of encouragement. But Clarence sat rigid in his chair, staring at Joey's back with an intensity that made my breath catch. His hand, still clutching his trumpet, was clenched into a white-knuckled fist.

In that moment, I feared that this wouldn't end with music.

Chapter Seven

As the intermission continued, the theater buzzed with animated conversation. I excused myself from James and Deputy O'Brien, intending to stretch my legs, when Vivian Ashford moved purposefully toward the backstage area.

The determined set of her shoulders and the flush in her cheeks told me exactly what she had in mind. I quickened my pace and intercepted her just before she reached the corridor leading to the green room.

"Vivian, sweetie." I touched her elbow. "Wasn't that magnificent?"

Her eyes flashed bright with excitement and something more dangerous—infatuation. "Oh, Miss Parrish! Yes, it was marvelous. I simply must tell Joey—Mr. Serpentine—how much I enjoyed his performance. I thought I'd just pop backstage for a moment—"

"I'm not sure that's wise." Resting my hand on her shoulder, I steered her back toward the auditorium. "The musicians are likely preparing for the second half, and Mr. Serpentine strikes me as someone who needs absolute concentration before a performance."

"But I only want a moment," she protested, though her steps had slowed. "Just to congratulate him."

I chose my next words carefully, keeping my tone kind but firm. "Vivian, may I speak frankly? You're a lovely young woman with excellent prospects. But there's something you should understand about men like Joey Serpentine."

She looked at me with wide, uncertain eyes. Kathleen brushed past us, carrying a large basket on her arm. I stayed focused on Vivian.

"Men of his caliber are pursued constantly," I continued. "In every town, at every performance, there are young women who want to catch his attention. The ones who succeed aren't the ones who chase—they're the ones who remain mysterious, just out of reach."

She wavered. Pride warring with desire, no doubt.

"Besides," I said, "he's surrounded by his fellow musicians right now, and I doubt he'd appreciate being interrupted during his preparations. You wouldn't want him to remember you as an inconvenience, would you?"

That struck home. Vivian's shoulders sagged. "I suppose you're right. I just thought... well, never mind what I thought."

"Why don't you return to your seat?" I suggested. "Enjoy the rest of the performance. If Mr. Serpentine is interested in renewing your acquaintance, he knows perfectly well how to find you. Men prefer to do the chasing, you know. It's in their nature."

Vivian managed a small smile. "You're very wise, Miss Parrish. Thank you for saving me from making a fool of myself."

She returned to her companions, and I made my way backstage to find out what Kathleen was up to.

The narrow corridor behind the stage smelled of dust, greasepaint, and decades of performances. The musicians' voices floated out from the green room, along with a familiar laugh that made me stop short.

Kathleen was holding court among the Midnight Serpents when I pushed the door open, the basket at her feet and a large spoon in her hand, scooping hefty servings of something into my best glass dessert dishes. I caught the scent of apples and cinnamon and guessed it was her famous apple cobbler. Sal, Sweet Lou, and Norman were enthusiastically consuming the dessert, making appreciative noises between bites.

"Mrs. Mulroney, you're a goddess," Sal declared around a mouthful of dessert. "This is even better than what you served last night."

"Oh, go on," Kathleen protested, but she was positively glowing with pleasure. "It's just a little something I whipped up. You boys were so complimentary about my cooking yesterday evening, I wanted to do something nice for you, help you keep up your strength. Besides, I needed to use the rest of the apples. So many apples this time of year."

I rolled my eyes, knowing for a fact there hadn't been a single apple left in my kitchen on Saturday morning. She must have dashed to the grocery for a fresh supply while I was at work. Despite this blatant untruth, I couldn't help but smile at her well-meant gesture.

Joey had returned from glad-handing the audience and stood slightly apart from the others, his golden trumpet resting on a nearby table. He gave Kathleen a grateful smile but shook his head when she offered him a dish.

"I promise you it doesn't contain any anise." Her expression was earnest, her tone pleading. "I felt so terrible when you couldn't enjoy last night's torte that I made this especially for you. And for the other boys, of course. But especially for you."

"Mrs. Mulroney, you are an angel," he said. "That looks delicious, but I never eat durin' a concert. I do my best playin' on an empty stomach."

"Oh, of course!" Kathleen looked disappointed, then rallied. "How about I wrap a portion for you? You could have it later, as a bedtime snack."

"That would be real nice of you."

Kathleen produced a sheet of waxed paper from her basket with the efficiency of a magician pulling a rabbit from a hat, then carefully wrapped a dishful of dessert with practiced hands, along with a spoon—one of Grandma Parrish's silver spoons, freshly polished. She handed the packet to Joey, who accepted it with a slight bow.

"You're too good to us," he said. "I'll look forward to enjoying this later tonight."

"Kathleen," I said from the doorway, making my presence known. "I might have guessed I'd find you here."

She turned with a start, though her expression was unrepentant. "Amanda! I was just—"

"Being characteristically generous," I finished. "Though I'm sure the musicians need to prepare for the second half."

"Of course, of course," Kathleen said. "We'll leave you gentlemen to your work and come back for the dishes later. Good lu—I mean, break a leg!" She threw me a triumphant glance at her deft use of the phrase.

We returned to our seats just as the houselights dimmed for the second half of the performance. My attention was divided between the music and the various dramas playing out in the audience. Vivian had somehow managed to position herself at the edge of the stage during intermission, and I watched with growing concern as she gazed up limpet-eyed at Joey Serpentine as though he were Adonis himself.

Poor Ezra Coldwell slipped out during the middle of a particularly energetic number, his face grim with defeat. Several of his most devoted students were dancing enthusiastically in the aisles, apparently converted to the jazz gospel in the span of a single evening.

The performance concluded to thunderous applause, with Joey taking multiple bows and blowing kisses to the ladies in the front row. As the audience filed out, conversations erupted on all sides—some thrilled, others scandalized, all talking about the band's impact on their quiet town.

"Well." James navigated our way toward the exit. "I don't think Timber Coulee will be quite the same after tonight."

"No," I agreed, watching Vivian push through the crowd toward the stage where Joey was packing his precious trumpet. "I'm afraid it won't."

Because something about the evening's events had left me with the uncomfortable feeling that the Midnight Serpents had brought more than just music to our town. They'd brought change, conflict, and the kind of dangerous excitement that usually ended badly for someone.

The audience spilled out into the chilly October night, their voices bright with excitement about the music they'd heard. Kathleen tugged at my sleeve.

"Come on. We need to retrieve those dishes before someone mistakes them for theater props. I'll never forgive myself if I lose your dishes and Grandma's good silver."

I'd never forgive her, either. I followed her through the side door that led backstage, weaving past stagehands breaking down music stands and gathering up scattered programs. The backstage area was cramped and shadowy, lit only by a few hanging bulbs that cast long shadows across the concrete floor.

The musicians were in various stages of packing up—brass instruments being swabbed dry, sheet music shuffled into folders, valve oil bottles being capped and tucked away. The air smelled of metal and cork grease, with an underlying scent of sweat and something sharper—the remnant of nerves and adrenaline.

Sweet Lou was carefully wrapping his trombone in a green cloth that looked suspiciously like a Pullman blanket. Norman sat on an overturned crate, polishing his saxophone with meticulous attention. Sal organized his drumsticks with the precision of a jeweler arranging gemstones.

"There they are," Kathleen said with relief, pointing to the jumble of dessert dishes and my good silverware on a table near the back wall. "Still intact, thank heavens."

I helped her gather everything, wrapping the forks and spoons in a tea towel while she stacked the plates in her basket. I pointed to a small portion of cobbler left in the serving dish. "Molly will appreciate that. Or I will, if I get to it first."

The atmosphere in the room was a strange mixture of exhaustion and exhilaration, with an undercurrent of tension that hadn't quite dissipated. Joey stood near his trumpet case, his back to us, carefully working the valves with a small bottle of oil. Even in this mundane moment, there was something theatrical about him—the way he held himself, the deliberate grace of his movements.

Movement in the deeper shadows caught my eye. Someone was standing just beyond the reach of the lights, half-hidden behind a stack of old set pieces. The silhouette was unmistakably feminine—the curve of a fashionable dress, the tilt of a head crowned with marcel waves.

Vivian Ashford.

She wasn't looking at me. Her entire focus was trained on Joey, and even from across the room, I read the longing in her posture, the way she leaned slightly forward as if drawn by an invisible thread.

"Amanda?" Kathleen's voice pulled me back. "Are you ready?"

"Almost," I murmured, not wanting to draw attention to myself as I observed the silent drama unfolding.

Vivian took a step forward into the half-light. She'd topped her evening dress with a deep green coat, her hair still perfectly coiffed despite the evening's exertions.

Joey must have sensed her presence because he turned, his expression shifting from tired satisfaction to something more guarded.

I was about to follow Kathleen out when Clarence appeared in the doorway, nearly colliding with us both.

"Pardon me, Mrs. Mulroney, Amanda," he mumbled, his face still pale from his earlier humiliation but his jaw set with determination. He looked past us to Joey. "Mr. Serpentine, might I have a word?"

The room fell silent. Sweet Lou and Norman exchanged glances while Sal openly stared. Joey's expression remained neutral, though I detected a flicker of wariness in his eyes.

Clarence's prominent Adam's-apple bobbed in his throat. He stepped forward and extended his hand. "I wanted to congratulate you on your performance earlier. That was... well, it was extraordinary. I've never heard anyone play like that."

For a moment, Joey simply looked at the offered hand. Then, slowly, he reached out and clasped it firmly.

"No hard feelings, I hope," Clarence continued. "It was good sportsmanship, challenging you like that. I learned something valuable tonight about the difference between technical skill and true artistry."

Something in Joey's expression softened. "You got solid technique, kid. That's a good foundation. Maybe you just need to learn when to let go of the rules and trust yourself."

They shook hands with what appeared to be genuine respect, as I reassessed both men. Clarence for having the courage to face his defeat gracefully, and Joey for accepting the olive branch when he could have easily twisted the knife further.

Kathleen nudged me, and I realized I'd been standing frozen, watching the exchange with undisguised interest. We started for the door, dishes carefully balanced between us.

Behind us, Clarence made his farewells, his footsteps echoing as he headed back toward the main theater. The other musicians seemed to take this as their cue to finish packing, their voices rising in casual conversation about the next day's travel plans.

I glanced back one more time as we reached the doorway.

Vivian had emerged fully from the shadows now and was approaching Joey with careful, deliberate steps. Her hands were clasped in front of her, and even from behind, I could see the tension in her shoulders, the hopeful tilt of her head.

Joey saw her coming. His expression, which had been almost warm during his exchange with Clarence, shuttered closed like a door slamming shut.

"We really should go," I murmured to Kathleen, but I couldn't quite tear my eyes away.

Vivian reached Joey and said something I couldn't hear. Her hand lifted slightly, as if she might touch his arm, but the gesture died incomplete. Joey's response was brief—just a few words and a subtle shake of his head.

The change in Vivian was instantaneous and devastating. Her shoulders drew up, her head dropped, and even in the dim light, I could see her hand lift to her face. When she turned away from Joey, I caught a glimpse of her profile—the shimmer of tears on her cheeks, the trembling of her chin.

She rushed past us without seeming to see us at all, one hand pressed to her mouth, the other clutching her coat closed. Her heels clicked rapidly against the concrete floor, the sound growing fainter as she fled toward the stage door that led to the alley.

"Oh my," Kathleen breathed. "That poor girl."

I looked back at Joey. He stood motionless, staring at the space where Vivian had been, his trumpet forgotten in his hands. For just a moment, his carefully constructed façade cracked, and something that might have been regret flickered across his features.

Then Sweet Lou called out, "Hey, Joey," and the mask slipped back into place. Joey turned away, bent to close his trumpet case with practiced efficiency, and called, "Yeah, Lou, whaddya want?"

"Come along, Amanda." Kathleen tugged at my arm. "Whatever just happened, it's none of our business."

Molly joined us for the walk home. But as we made our way out into the chilly night, I couldn't shake the image of Vivian's tears or the way Joey had closed himself off so completely. There was a story there—a history written in the space between them, in the plea in her eyes and the steel in his refusal.

A story that, I suspected, wasn't finished yet.

The stage door clanged shut behind us, and I pulled my coat tighter against the chill. Somewhere in the darkness, a woman was crying over a man who wouldn't—or couldn't—return her affection.

Chapter Eight

As church bells tolled their merry call across Timber Coulee, summoning the faithful to worship, I sat between Kathleen and Molly in my usual spot—fourth row from the front, left side. Often James sat with me unless, like this morning, he was on duty. Clarence sat up front with the rest of the choir. The congregation filled in around us with the comfortable rustle of Sunday best and hushed greetings.

After the opening hymns and prayers, Reverend Miller took his place at the pulpit, his kind face grave with concern. He was a tall, lean man in his fifties, with wire-rimmed spectacles and a gentle manner that made even his sternest warnings feel like the worried counsel of a beloved uncle.

"My dear brothers and sisters." His voice carried easily through the sanctuary, "I come before you this morning with a heavy heart, compelled to speak on a matter that troubles many of us deeply."

Beside me, Kathleen shifted slightly. On my other side, Molly's hands stilled on her hymnal.

"There is a tide rising in our nation," Reverend Miller continued, "a cultural force that enters our homes through Tin Pan Alley, through the phonograph, through the very air of our modern age. I speak, of course, of this new music they call jazz."

A murmur rippled through the congregation. I kept my eyes fixed on the reverend, though I could feel Martha Barrington's gaze burning into the back of my head from three rows behind.

"Now, I know some of you may think me old-fashioned," A slight smile softened his words. "Perhaps you believe I simply don't understand the appeal of modern music. But I ask you to consider not the melody, but the message. Not the rhythm, but the result."

He paused, removing his spectacles to clean them, no doubt choosing his next words with care.

"This jazz music comes from the speakeasies and dance halls of our great cities. It is born in places where the law is flouted and morals are cast aside. It carries with it the spirit of rebellion, of excess, of—forgive my plain speaking—of sensuality that has no place in the lives of our young people."

I paid close attention, despite my reservations. Reverend Miller was no fire-and-brimstone preacher, ranting about damnation. He was a shepherd worried for his flock.

His voice grew more earnest. "I see our young people, good boys and girls from solid Christian homes, and I watch as this music changes them. The way they dress, the way they speak, the way they move. They stay out later. They become restless with the simple, wholesome pleasures that sustained their parents. They hunger for excitement, for novelty, for experiences that pull them away from family, from faith, from everything we hold dear."

He replaced his spectacles and gripped the edges of the pulpit.

"I do not speak from ignorance or fear of change. I speak from observation, from the counsel I've given to worried parents, from the tears of mothers who no longer recognize their own children. This music—this jazz—it is not merely entertainment. It is a doorway to a world that will consume our young people if we do not stand firm."

Kathleen's hand found mine and squeezed. I squeezed back, unsure whether she was offering comfort or seeking it.

"I am not calling for hatred or judgment." The reverend's tone gentled. "I am calling for vigilance. For wisdom. For the courage to say 'no' when the world around us shouts 'yes.' Our young people need guidance, not condemnation. They need us to show them a better way, to remind them that the old paths are not outdated—they are the ones that lead to life, to peace, to joy that doesn't fade when the music stops."

He bowed his head briefly, then looked up with that warm, concerned expression that made him so beloved in the community.

"Let us be careful, my friends, about what we allow into our homes, into our hearts. Let us remember that we are called to be in the world, but not of it. And let us pray for our young people, that they might have the strength to resist the allure of a culture that promises everything but delivers only emptiness."

The sermon continued for another ten minutes, but my mind wandered. I thought of my shop, of the jazz records I'd ordered because my customers wanted them, of how well they were selling. I thought of the joy on young people's faces when they found the latest recording. Was that joy empty? Was it leading them astray?

I didn't have the answers. But I couldn't quite accept Reverend Miller's conclusions, even as I respected his concern.

As the service concluded and people left their pews, I stood and smoothed my Sunday dress—a modest blue crepe with a white collar that Molly had helped me choose. We moved toward the aisle, joining the slow procession toward the doors where Reverend Miller stood greeting his flock.

We had barely made it three pews when Martha Barrington intercepted us.

Martha was a formidable woman in her sixties, dressed in an elaborate purple suit with a hat that featured no fewer than three feathers. Her face was set in lines of perpetual disapproval, and her eyes—sharp and gray—fixed on me with the precision of a hawk spotting prey.

"Amanda Parrish." Her voice carried across the departing congregation. Several heads turned. "I hope you were listening carefully to Reverend Miller's sermon this morning."

My stomach tightened, but I kept my expression pleasant. "Good morning, Martha. Yes, it was a thought-provoking message."

"Thought-provoking?" Her eyebrows rose dramatically. "It was a clear warning, and one that some people in this town would do well to heed." She stepped closer, lowering her voice only slightly. "I understand from my Rodney you're still selling those jazz records in your shop. In spite of everything Reverend Miller just said about the corrupting influence of that so-called music!"

Molly's hand touched my elbow—a silent gesture of support.

"I sell all kinds of music, Martha," I said evenly. "Classical, hymns, popular songs—"

"But you stock jazz," she interrupted. "You make it available to our young people. You profit from their corruption."

Heat rose in my cheeks, but before I could respond, another voice cut through the tension.

"Oh, for heaven's sake, Martha."

Heidi Fischer materialized at my side like a guardian angel in a sensible gray suit. Heidi was my friend, the owner of Elite Repeat and possessor of a sharp mind and an even sharper tongue when the situation called for it. Her blue eyes flashed with annoyance.

"Amanda runs a business," Heidi continued, "not a church. She sells what people want to buy. That's called commerce, not corruption."

Martha drew herself up to her full height. "And you, Heidi Fischer, are exactly the kind of modern woman Reverend Miller was warning about. No respect for tradition, no concern for—"

"I have tremendous respect for tradition," Heidi said calmly. "I carry vintage and traditional objects in my shop every day. But I also believe in freedom and personal responsibility. If you don't want jazz music in your home, don't buy it. But don't expect everyone else to live by your particular convictions."

"They are not *my* convictions—they're the truth!" Martha's voice rose.

"It's Reverend Miller's interpretation," Heidi corrected. "Which is not quite the same thing."

A small crowd had gathered now, watching the exchange with poorly concealed interest. I wanted nothing more than to disappear through the church floor.

"Ladies," Molly interjected, "perhaps this isn't the best place—"

"I'm simply trying to protect this community." Martha's face flushed crimson. "Unlike some people, I care about the souls of our young people."

"And I care about treating my neighbors with respect and not judging their businesses or their choices," Heidi shot back.

"Heidi, please." I touched her arm. "It's all right."

"It's not all right." But she lowered her voice. "You have every right to run your shop as you see fit."

Martha made a sound somewhere between a sniff and a snort. "Mark my words, Amanda Parrish. This jazz business will bring nothing but trouble to Timber Coulee. And when it does, don't expect any sympathy from those of us who tried to warn you."

With that pronouncement, she swept away, her feathers bobbing indignantly.

At last, I exhaled.

"Thank you," I said to Heidi, "but you didn't need to—"

"Yes, I did." She gave a firm nod. "Martha Barrington has been the self-appointed moral guardian of this town for too long. Someone needs to remind her that she doesn't speak for all of us." She relaxed a little. "Are you all right?"

"I'm fine." Although my hands were trembling slightly. "Just not used to being the center of controversy on a Sunday morning."

"Well, get used to it." Heidi's smile was wry. "Surely you know by now that running a business in this town—especially one that sells anything remotely modern—you're going to ruffle feathers. Particularly Mrs. Barrington's rather elaborate ones."

"She caught me off guard, that's all." Despite everything, I smiled.

We continued toward the door, where Reverend Miller still greeted worshipers. When I reached him, his expression was apologetic.

"Miss Parrish." He took my hand. "I hope my sermon didn't cause you any distress."

"Not at all, Reverend," I said honestly. "You gave me a lot to think about."

"That's all I ask," he said. "I know your music shop serves the community well. I only hope you'll consider carefully what you're introducing into people's homes."

"I always do, Reverend."

He squeezed my hand and turned to greet Kathleen and Molly.

The walk home was quiet at first. The afternoon sun was warm for October, and the streets of Timber Coulee were peaceful in that particular Sunday way—shops closed, families gathering for Sunday dinner, the week's labors temporarily forgotten.

"Well," Molly said finally, "that was quite a morning."

"I'm sorry," I said. "I didn't mean to cause a scene."

"You didn't cause anything." Kathleen's tone was firm. "That Mrs. Barrington caused a scene. You just stood there."

"Heidi was wonderful," Molly added. "I've always liked her."

We turned onto our street, where the sheriff's automobile parked in front of my house.

My heart sank. A visit from Sheriff James Holcomb while he was on duty could only mean one thing. Something was amiss.

James leaned against the Dodge, his hat in his hands. When he saw us approaching, he straightened, shoulders tense, the expression on his handsome face carefully controlled.

"James?" I quickened my pace. "What's happened?"

He waited until we were closer before speaking, his eyes moving from me to Kathleen to Molly and back again.

"I'm afraid I have some bad news. Joey Serpentine was found dead in his hotel room early this morning."

The words seemed to hang in the air. The world tilted.

"Dead? What do you mean, dead?" Molly's face paled, and I threw an arm around her shoulder to steady her.

"But... how?" Kathleen's voice was barely a whisper. " What happened?"

James's expression was grave but kindhearted. "It appears to be a severe reaction to something he ate. On the surface it looks like a terrible accident. He ingested something he shouldn't have. An ambulance was called by hotel staff, but when the crew got there, he was already gone."

"Oh, no." Molly sounded as if she'd had the wind knocked out of her. "Poor Joey."

I frowned at James. "You said 'on the surface.' You mean it might not have been an accident?"

He drew a breath. "There was evidence he'd eaten something before bed—the remains of a dessert. Given the discussion at dinner Friday night about his allergy to anise, I need to ask you, Kathleen, about the ingredients in the dish you made for the band."

The color drained from Kathleen's face. "Oh, my stars."

"Let's go inside." Molly unlocked the door. "We shouldn't discuss this on the street."

We filed into the parlor, and I moved automatically, taking James's hat, gesturing him toward a chair. Kathleen sank onto the sofa as if her legs wouldn't hold her, and Molly sat beside her, taking her hand.

James remained standing as he pulled a small notebook from his jacket pocket. His manner was professional, but concern lingered in his eyes when he looked at Kathleen.

"I know this is difficult, but I need to establish the facts." His voice was kind. "Kathleen, you brought dessert to the concert last night, is that correct?"

"Yes." Kathleen's voice shook. "Apple cobbler. I made it yesterday afternoon, brought it to the theater, and gave it to the band at intermission. The band members had been so complimentary about my cooking at dinner the night before, I wanted to... I wanted to do something nice for them."

James made a note. "What ingredients did you use? I need a complete list."

Kathleen closed her eyes, clearly trying to remember. "Apples, sugar, a little lemon juice and cinnamon. And a touch of ground cloves. For the topping, I used oats, flour, brown sugar, and butter. Just those ingredients, I swear it. No anise, no licorice flavoring, nothing like that. I was so careful, James. After what Joey said at dinner about his allergy, I was so careful."

"I believe you," James said in a calm voice. "But you're absolutely certain? You didn't add any spices that might have contained anise? No star anise in the spice cabinet that might have gotten mixed up with something else?"

"Amanda doesn't even own star anise, just anise extract. She's not much of a cook." That last comment seemed unnecessary, but given the circumstances, I let it go. A single tear trickled down my sister's face. "I would never—I knew he could die from it. I would never have put it in anything I made for him."

"And Joey Serpentine ate some of this cobbler?" James asked.

Kathleen blinked. "Why, no. Not in my presence, at least. He said he never eats during a concert—it affects his playing or something—but he'd enjoy it afterward." Kathleen's hands twisted in her lap. "He seemed so pleased. He said it looked delicious."

Her voice broke on the last word, and Molly pulled her closer.

I sat on Kathleen's other side and took her hand. James seemed to struggle between his duty as sheriff and his care for the people in this room.

"James," I prompted, "what exactly happened? Are you saying Joey died from anise in the dessert?"

James hesitated. "It looks that way. Dr. Moriarty examined the body. All signs point to a severe allergic reaction—anaphylaxis. There were whiffs of what appears to be ground anise seed or anise extract in the remains of the dessert found in Joey's room. And the flavor was there—the doctor tasted it." He looked at Kathleen. "I'm not accusing you of anything, Kathleen. I know you just met Joey, and you had no reason to wish him harm. But if indeed he died from an allergic reaction, I need to understand how anise got into that dessert."

"I don't know." Her tears flowed freely now. "I don't know. I didn't put it there. I swear I didn't."

"Could someone else have tampered with it?" Molly asked. "After my mother made it?"

James's expression shifted, becoming more thoughtful. "That's a possibility we're exploring. Kathleen, after you brought the desserts to the theater, were they left unattended at any point?"

Kathleen wiped her eyes, trying to think. "I... I don't remember. I brought them backstage during intermission. The band members were there. Everyone took one except Joey, who said he'd save his for later. I think... I think he set it aside on a table? Then we all went back out for the second half of the concert."

"So anyone backstage would have had access to Joey's portion." James wrote in his notebook.

"But who would do such a thing?" I asked. "And why?"

James met my eyes, and the answer was there. He didn't know, but he intended to find out.

"There's one way to check," I said. "There was some cobbler left over. We brought it home last night. It should be in the icebox."

"No, it's not." Molly dipped her head, sheepish. "I polished it off this morning before church, while I was waiting for you two to finish getting ready." She squeezed Kathleen's shoulders. "It was delicious, Mother. One of your best."

James scratched something in his notebook. "Did you taste any anise in it?"

"I don't know. I'm not sure." She brightened. "But maybe we can find out. The serving dish is still in the sink, waiting to be washed."

Even through her tears, Kathleen's expression turned indignant. "You left a dirty dish in the sink?"

"Let's stay focused." I made a beeline for the kitchen, the other three close behind. There sat the cobbler-encrusted dish, right there in the sink. Never had I been so pleased that Molly wasn't much of a housekeeper. I grabbed a spoon, scraped at the remnants of cobbler, and took a taste.

"Well?" Kathleen demanded. "Is there anise in it?"

I took another nibble. My spirit lifted. "I don't taste any. But I can't say for sure. It's subtle sometimes."

"Give that to me." Kathleen grabbed the dish and a clean spoon. She scraped up some crust and put it on her tongue. A cloud of disappointment swept over her face. "I can't tell for sure, either. But if there *is* anise in there, I know *I* didn't put it there."

James took hold of the dish. "I'll take this with me. We can have it tested in the lab and find out for sure."

"How long will that take?"

"Well, the lab's not open on Sunday. But I can take it into Spokane first thing tomorrow and ask them to put a rush on it. We should have the results by Tuesday, if not sooner."

Kathleen had stopped crying. "And if it's free of anise? As I'm sure it is?"

"Then we will know someone purposely added anise to Joey's portion," I said.

"In which case, this turns Mr. Serpentine's death from an accident to something much more serious." James set the dish on the counter and picked up his notebook. "If the lab results confirm that the original dessert contained no anise, but Joey's portion did, I'll need to interview everyone who was at the theater last night. The band members, anyone who had access backstage and might have tampered with it." He looked at Kathleen, his expression softening. "I know this is devastating, and I'm sorry. But I need to ask—is there anything else you can remember? Anything unusual about last night at the theater?"

Kathleen collapsed onto a kitchen chair and shook her head. "Nothing. Everyone was so happy, so excited about the concert. Joey was wonderful—his solo was beautiful. And now he's..." She couldn't finish the sentence.

James closed his notebook, then crouched down to Kathleen's eye level. "Listen to me. I don't believe you did this intentionally, and I don't think anyone else will either. But I need you to go through everything in your mind, write down every detail you can remember about making that dessert and what happened to it after it left your kitchen. Can you do that for me?"

Kathleen nodded, sniffling.

James stood, and I walked him to the door. On the threshold, he paused, speaking so only I could hear.

"Amanda, I meant what I said. I don't think Kathleen had anything to do with this. But, pending the lab results, someone did. Someone who knew about Joey's allergy, who had access to that dessert, and who wanted Joey Serpentine dead." His jaw tightened. "I'm going to find out who."

"Be careful," I said. "If someone killed Joey deliberately, they might not stop at one person."

James's hand found mine, squeezed briefly. "You be careful too. Until we know what happened and why, I want you, your sister, and Molly to be extra cautious."

"But I want to help," I insisted. "My sister's reputation is at stake."

He settled his hat on his head. "We won't know anything conclusive until we get the lab results. But there's no reason we can't ask a few questions, starting with the band." He looked at me as if weighing something in his mind. "Want to come along?"

"I'll get my coat."

From the kitchen, I could hear Kathleen's sniffles and Molly's soft, comforting murmurs. The morning's controversy over jazz records seemed trivial now, almost absurd. Mrs. Barrington had been wrong about one thing—the trouble that had come to Timber Coulee hadn't been brought by music.

It may have been brought by murder.

Chapter Nine

The drive to the sheriff's office was brief but tense. James stared straight ahead, the cobbler dish wrapped carefully in a tea towel on the seat between us. The streets were quiet, most families still gathered around Sunday dinner tables, blissfully unaware that a famous musician lay dead at the Timber Coulee Hotel.

"I appreciate your letting me come along," I said as we pulled away from the curb.

"You have a stake in this." James fixed his eyes on the road. "And you notice things other people miss. I'd be foolish not to take advantage of that." He paused as we turned onto Main Street. "Besides, the band members know you. They might be more comfortable talking with you present."

He parked in front of the modest brick building that housed both the sheriff's office and a single jail cell. He retrieved the cobbler dish, and we went inside.

The office smelled faintly of coffee and old paper. Deputy Peterson sat at his desk, holding a telephone receiver to his ear. Deputy Margaret O'Brien occupied a desk near the window, bent over a file with intense concentration. She looked up as we entered, and I was struck again by how different she was from the matronly prison guard I'd imagined when James first mentioned her.

She'd changed out of the dress she'd worn to the concert the previous night and into her crisp uniform, the deputy's badge gleaming on her jacket. Her blond hair was pinned in a neat bun, and those striking blue eyes that had assessed the crowd at the concert now focused on James with obvious respect.

"Sheriff." She stood. "Miss Parrish."

"Deputy O'Brien." James lifted a hand in greeting. "Working on the Gunderson case?"

"Yes, sir. Going through the witness statements again. I think there might be an inconsistency in the timeline that could—" She looked at me and caught herself. "But that can wait. Is there something you need?"

James set the wrapped dish on his desk. "I need you to take this to the Spokane lab first thing tomorrow morning. Ask them to test for the presence of anise—specifically, to determine whether ground anise seed or maybe anise extract was mixed into this dessert."

Deputy O'Brien's eyebrows rose with interest. "This relates to Mr. Serpentine's death?"

"Possibly." James unlocked the evidence cabinet and carefully placed the dish inside. "On the surface, it appears Mr. Serpentine died from an allergic reaction after consuming a dessert that may have contained anise. But we need to determine whether the anise was in the original dessert or if it was added to his portion specifically."

"And if it was added specifically—" Deputy O'Brien's eyes widened with understanding. "Then we're looking at something far more serious than an accident."

"Exactly. Which is why we need those results as quickly as possible. Can you have them rush it?"

"I'll make sure they understand the urgency." Deputy O'Brien pulled out her notebook and jotted a note. "Is there anything else I can do to assist?"

"Not at the moment. For now, we're treating this as a tragic accident unless the lab results indicate otherwise. No need to alarm anyone or interfere with other cases." James glanced at me, then back to his deputy. "But I would appreciate your joining Miss Parrish and me at the hotel. We're going to speak with the band members, and it wouldn't hurt to have an extra set of eyes and ears. Deputy Peterson here can hold down the fort, can't you, Deputy?"

Deputy Peterson, still on the telephone, made a half-salute gesture of acknowledgement.

"Of course, Sheriff." Deputy O'Brien retrieved her hat and settled it on her head. "I'm ready whenever you are."

As we walked the three blocks to the Timber Coulee Hotel, Deputy O'Brien fell into step beside James, and I trailed a bit behind, watching their easy professional rapport. She was explaining her thoughts on the Gunderson case—something about a disputed property line and conflicting testimony—and James listened with the focused attention he gave to all matters of law enforcement.

"The key is finding someone who can verify the original fence line." She gestured with one hand while the other held her notebook. "If we can establish where it was before Clyde moved it, we can prove his claim is fraudulent."

"Good thinking." James nodded his approval. "Follow up on that tomorrow after you return from Spokane."

I studied Deputy O'Brien as we walked. She was competent, clearly intelligent, and moved with an easy confidence. More than that, she seemed to enjoy her work, her eyes bright with enthusiasm as she discussed the intricacies of the case.

And she fit naturally into James's world—the world of investigations and evidence and legal procedures that I could only observe from the outside.

"Miss Parrish." Deputy O'Brien turned to include me in the conversation. "Did you enjoy the concert last night?"

"Yes, I did." Was it only just last night? It felt like days had passed since then.

"I was talking to somebody about your music shop," the deputy continued. "Sounds like your inventory is quite extensive for a town this size."

"Thank you." I was surprised by her attention to such details. "I try to serve the community's needs, though lately there's been some controversy about what those needs actually are."

"Ah, yes. The jazz records." A slight smile played at the corners of her mouth. "I noticed the tension during Reverend Miller's sermon this morning. Mrs. Barrington looked as if she might spontaneously combust when she spotted you."

"You were at church this morning?" I don't know why that surprised me.

"I try to attend when I can. It helps to understand a community's values and concerns." She glanced at James, then me. "Though I must say, the sermon seemed rather pointed. Do you face much opposition to your business practices?"

"Some," I said. "Mrs. Barrington believes I'm contributing to the moral degradation of the town's youth by selling modern music."

"While you believe you're simply meeting customer demand," Deputy O'Brien said. It wasn't a question, but a statement of understanding. "It's a delicate balance, isn't it? Serving the community while also pushing against outdated restrictions."

I thawed a bit toward her despite my earlier unease. She was perceptive, and her comments suggested she understood the complications of being a businesswoman in a small town.

The Timber Coulee Hotel rose before us, a three-story brick building that served as the town's finest accommodation for traveling businessmen and the occasional tourist. Mr. Cavanaugh, the manager, met us in the lobby, his usually jovial face drawn and haggard.

"Sheriff, Miss Parrish." He acknowledged us, and James introduced him to Deputy O'Brien. Mr. Cavanaugh shook the deputy's hand. "A terrible business, just terrible. Nothing like this has ever happened at my establishment. The band members are gathered in the dining room, which is closed to the public until this evening—I thought that would be more comfortable than having you interview them in their rooms."

"That was thoughtful, sir," James said. "Has anyone left the hotel since this morning?"

"No, sir. I haven't restricted anyone's movements, but they've all stayed close. I think they're in shock, to be honest. They keep asking questions I can't answer."

"We'll do our best to provide some clarity," James said.

Deputy O'Brien's pen scratched across her notebook. "We may need them to remain in Timber Coulee for a few days, depending on what we learn. But that's premature at this point."

Mr. Cavanaugh's eyebrows rose at her authoritative tone, but he nodded. "Of course, Deputy. I'll let the guests know if it becomes necessary."

He led us through the lobby to the hotel's dining room, where the remaining members of the Midnight Serpents sat around a large table. The cheerful camaraderie at Friday's dinner party had been replaced by a pall of shock and grief.

Norman sat with his head in his hands, his usually neat hair disheveled. Sweet Lou stared into a coffee cup, his handsome face haggard. Frank hunched over the table, his wire-rimmed spectacles askew, looking as if he might be sick. Sal was the only one who looked up as we entered, his big brown spaniel eyes red-rimmed but alert.

"Sheriff," Sal said. "Have you—is there any more information about what happened to Joey?"

James pulled out a chair and sat down, and Deputy O'Brien and I followed suit. The deputy positioned herself where she could observe all the band members.

"We're still gathering information." James's voice was calm and professional. "At this point, Dr. Moriarty has confirmed that Mr. Serpentine suffered a severe allergic reaction resulting in anaphylactic shock. It appears to be just an unfortunate accident, but we won't know more until we've completed our investigation. I know this is a difficult time, but I need to ask you some questions about last night. The more information we can gather now, the sooner we can understand what happened."

"We'll help however we can." Norman lifted his head. His eyes were damp. "Joey could be—well, he could be difficult. But he was our band-leader. Our friend." His voice cracked on the last word.

"Let's start with the basics," Deputy O'Brien said, her pen poised. "Can each of you account for your whereabouts from the end of the concert until you went to bed last night?"

Sweet Lou went first. "After the finale, I helped pack up the gear. Must've been around eleven o'clock when me and Frank drifted. Then I went back to my room, read for a spell, and fell asleep. Room twelve, second floor."

Frank spoke next, his voice barely above a whisper, his hands trembling slightly as he adjusted his spectacles. "Same. I helped pack up, then went to my room. Room fourteen, also second floor. I felt restless, so I came back down and practiced some scales on the piano in the lobby until about midnight. Mr. Cavanaugh can probably confirm that."

"I can," Mr. Cavanaugh said from where he remained near the doorway. "I was working on the books in my office and could hear the piano. Very nice playing, I might add."

Frank's hands were still shaking as he clasped them together on the table. The poor man looked absolutely terrified, though whether from grief or from being questioned by law enforcement, it was hard to say.

Norman cleared his throat. "I stayed backstage a bit longer, talking with some folks who came to congratulate us on the performance. Local musi-cians, mostly, wanting to know about our arrangements. I got back to the hotel around eleven thirty, I'd say. Room nine, second floor." He paused. "Joey's room was right across the hall from mine. Room ten. I didn't hear anything unusual before I went to sleep. Then the ambulance woke me up around three."

"And you, Mr. Benedetti?" Deputy O'Brien asked, looking at Sal.

Sal shifted in his chair. "I packed the drums—that always takes the longest since there are so many pieces. Then I walked back to the hotel by myself. Must've been around eleven thirty, maybe? My room is seven, on the first floor." He rubbed his tired face. "I couldn't sleep right away. Kept thinkin' about—well, about a lotta things. The future of the band, mostly. Joey had mentioned wantin' to settle down, maybe open a club somewhere. The rest of us was worried about what that would mean for our livelihoods."

"Did Mr. Serpentine mention anything specific about his plans?" James asked.

"Not really. Just that he was tired of travelin', wanted to put down roots." Sal's expression darkened. "Joey was always thinkin' about Joey, you know? The rest of us just had to figure out how to make our own plans around his."

"That's not fair, Sal." Norman's voice was hoarse. "He carried the band. We all knew that."

"Carryin' the band and carin' about the band are two different things," Sal muttered. Then tears came to his eyes. "I'm sorry. I shouldn't speak ill of the dead. Joey was family, and I'm—I'm devastated that he's gone." His face hardened. "Although what a knucklehead—eatin' somethin' that'd kill him. Shoulda been more careful."

I watched the exchange carefully, noting the complicated grief in Sal's voice, one moment sad, the next moment angry. Losing a family member was always difficult, especially when the relationship had been strained.

"When was the last time each of you saw Mr. Serpentine alive?" Deputy O'Brien asked.

"At the theater, right after the concert," Sweet Lou said. The others nodded in agreement.

"He was accepting congratulations from the audience," Norman added. "He loved that part—the applause, the attention. We all left before he did.

Joey always liked to be the last one to leave, make sure everyone knew he was the star."

Frank's hands tightened on the table. "He—he wouldn't let me leave until I'd wiped down every key on the piano. Said I'd left fingerprints on the ivory and it looked unprofessional." His voice was bitter. "Even at the end, he couldn't just let us do our jobs without criticism."

I studied Frank more closely. The young pianist seemed truly distressed, but there was anger mixed with the grief—resentment that had clearly been building for some time.

"Did any of you return to his room later? Perhaps to discuss the next day's schedule or travel plans?" James asked.

The band members exchanged glances, and something passed between them—a shared knowledge, perhaps, or a shared secret.

"No," Frank said quickly—too quickly. "We all went to our own rooms. Joey preferred to be alone after performances. He said the music kept playing in his head, and he needed silence to let it fade."

But his trembling hands and the way his eyes darted toward Sal suggested there might be more to the story.

"Did Mr. Serpentine have anyone who might have wished him harm?" James asked carefully. "I'm not suggesting anything sinister, you understand—just trying to get a complete picture of his relationships."

The silence that followed was heavy with unspoken thoughts.

Finally Norman spoke. "Joey rubbed some people the wrong way. He could be arrogant, dismissive. Especially to Frank—sorry, Frankie, but it's true. Joey rode you pretty hard."

Frank's face flushed. "He rode all of us hard. That's just how he was."

"But some folks took it harder than others," Sweet Lou said. "Fingers, you nearly quit the band in Spokane. We all remember that."

"I was frustrated," Frank said defensively. "Joey kept changing the arrangements at the last minute, expecting me to sight-read complex chord progressions with no warning. But I didn't—I wouldn't—" He couldn't seem to finish the sentence.

"No one is accusing you of anything." Deputy O'Brien's voice was kind yet firm. "We're simply trying to understand Mr. Serpentine's relationships with the people around him."

"What about that girl?" Sal said, seeming eager to shift attention away from Frank. "The one from Spokane who showed up here in town. Vivian somethin'?"

My stomach tightened. I'd been dreading this. "Vivian Ashford."

The deputy looked at me. "The girl who works at the general store?"

I nodded.

"She was at the concert last night," Sal continued. "Sittin' right in the front row, starin' at Joey like he was the Angel Gabriel. And she came backstage after the show too, didn't she? Tryin' to talk to him?"

"I saw her backstage briefly," Norman confirmed. "She tried to talk to Joey, but he brushed her off. Poor girl looked crushed."

Deputy O'Brien's pen paused. "Did Mr. Serpentine have a history with Miss Ashford?"

"They met after a concert in Spokane a few months back," Sweet Lou said. "Joey was—well, he came on pretty strong, like he does with dames in every town. Might've even taken her out on the town or whatever. But it was just Joey bein' Joey, you know? He never meant nothin' serious by it."

"I tried to tell Joey he needed to be more careful." Frustration roughened Sal's voice now. "You can't just charm every girl you meet and then act surprised when they think it means somethin'. But Joey never listened. He'd just laugh it off, say I was being too serious."

I thought of Vivian's desperate pursuit of Joey, her determination to help in my kitchen Friday night just to be near him, the tears on her face when he'd rejected her backstage after the concert. Had her infatuation curdled into something darker?

"We may need to speak with Miss Ashford." James made a note. "Is there anyone else who might have had a grievance against Mr. Serpentine?"

Another weighted silence.

"There was that young man at the concert." Frank hesitated. "The one who challenged Joey to the musical duel during intermission. He was at your dinner party, Miss Parrish. Clarence something? Joey humiliated him pretty badly in front of everyone."

"Clarence Butterworth." My voice came out sharper than I'd intended. "He's my niece's fiancé, and he was simply trying to be friendly by challenging Joey. It was meant as a gesture of respect, not competition."

"Joey didn't take it that way." Norman's tone was apologetic. "He saw it as a challenge to his dominance. And Joey never backed down from a challenge—he had to win, and he had to make sure everyone knew he'd won."

"Mr. Butterworth came backstage after the concert," I said. "He came to congratulate Joey and apologize for any offense. They shook hands. It was—it was actually quite gracious on both their parts."

"Gracious on the surface, maybe," Sal said. "But that Butterworth fella looked pretty sore to me. Being humiliated in front of your fiancée and the whole town? That's the kind of thing that can make a man do somethin' he might regret."

"Clarence wouldn't hurt anyone." I was firm on that score. "He's a gentle soul, a music teacher. The idea that he would—" I couldn't finish the sentence.

Deputy O'Brien's eyes met mine with sympathy. "I'm sure that's true, Miss Parrish. But if this does turn out to be more than an accident, we'll need to speak with everyone who had contact with Mr. Serpentine last night."

James shifted in his seat. "Let's talk about the dessert Mrs. Mulroney brought to the theater. Can any of you describe what happened to it after she delivered it backstage?"

"She brought a great big panful," Norman said, spreading his hands to indicate the enormity, "then spooned it into those little glass dessert dishes. Must have been five or six of them. She offered them around, and most of us took one right away. It was really kind of her—that cobbler was delicious."

"Joey said he'd save his for later," Sal added. "Said he never eats during a concert 'cause it affects his breath control or something. So he set his portion aside on that table in the green room, where we'd stacked some of our equipment cases."

"And then what happened?" Deputy O'Brien asked.

"We all went back out for the second half," Sweet Lou said. "The dessert was left in the green room. I guess anybody coulda gotten to it during the second half."

"Did you notice anyone going backstage who shouldn't have been there?" James asked.

The band members looked at each other and shrugged.

"It was chaos," Norman said. "Theater staff, well-wishers, people wanting autographs. The backstage area wasn't secured or anything. Anyone could have walked back there."

"Including the girl," Sweet Lou pointed out. "Vivian. She was lurkin' around after the concert. She definitely went backstage—I saw her headin' that direction."

My mind raced. Vivian had been in my kitchen Friday night. She'd heard Joey describe his allergy in detail. She'd been heartbroken when he rejected her after the concert. And she'd had access to the dessert backstage.

But could she really have done something so terrible? The Vivian I knew was a sweet, if somewhat naive, young woman with dreams of becoming a teacher. Not a murderer.

"I need to ask a question." Deputy O'Brien's tone was firm. "Did any of you know about Mr. Serpentine's allergy to anise before Friday's dinner party?"

"I did," Sal said. "We grew up together. Like I tole ya, he's my cousin. I was there when he had that reaction as a kid, at my ninth birthday party. Scared the heck out of all of us. Joey turned purple, couldn't breathe. We thought we were gonna lose him."

"But the rest of you?" Deputy O'Brien pressed.

Norman and Sweet Lou shook their heads. "Joey mentioned not liking certain foods, but he never told us about a serious allergy," Norman said. "Not until Friday night at dinner, when Mrs. Mulroney brought out that torte that had anise in it."

"Same here," Frank added. "I had no idea it was that serious. I just thought he was picky about food."

So the list of people who knew about the allergy before Friday's dinner was very short. And after Friday's dinner, it included everyone at my cottage that night—the band members, Clarence, Vivian, James, Molly, Kathleen, and myself.

"One more question," James said. "Did any of you go to Mr. Serpentine's hotel room after the concert? Perhaps to check on him, or to continue discussing band business?"

Frank clasped his hands. Norman and Sweet Lou both shook their heads.

Sal opened his mouth, then closed it again. A flicker of something—hesitation?—crossed his face.

"Sal?" Deputy O'Brien cocked her head. "Did you visit Mr. Serpentine's room?"

"I—yeah," Sal admitted. "But not for long. I had a question about the next stop on the tour. So I went up to his room, knocked on his door. He let me in, and we talked for a few minutes."

"What did you talk about?" James asked.

"Nothin' important. Band stuff. His plans for maybe settlin' down. I told him Mrs. Mulroney would be disappointed if he didn't eat her cobbler." Sal's voice was matter-of-fact. "I joked about her hauntin' him if he didn't eat it all. Then he started yawnin', so I left."

"Did he eat the dessert while you were there?"

"No. It was still sittin' on his nightstand when I left."

"What time was this?" Deputy O'Brien asked, writing rapidly.

"Maybe midnight? Somewhere around there."

"And you didn't return to his room after that?"

"No. I went to bed and stayed there, until the ambulance siren woke me up." Sal met Deputy O'Brien's gaze steadily. "Joey was family. We had our differences, sure, but he was still family."

I studied Sal's face as he spoke. He looked honestly distraught, his broad features etched with grief. The loss of a family member, even a difficult one, was never easy.

"No one is suggesting anything inappropriate, Mr. Benedetti," James said. "We're simply trying to establish the timeline of events. Did you notice anything unusual in Mr. Serpentine's room? Anything out of place?"

"No. It was just Joey being Joey—clothes everywhere, his trumpet case open on the dresser, sheet music scattered around. He was never tidy."

"That's enough for now," James said. "Thank you all for your cooperation. Depending on what we learn over the next few days, we may have additional questions. For now, you're free to go about your business, though we'd appreciate it if you remained in Timber Coulee for the time being."

"What about our bookings?" Norman asked anxiously. "We have contracts, obligations—"

"Let's wait and see what we learn," James said. "If it becomes necessary for you to stay longer, we'll work with your booking agent to explain the circumstances."

As we prepared to leave, Frank watched me with an odd intensity. When our eyes met, he looked away, his face flushing with what might have been embarrassment or—fear.

Outside the hotel, the moon was rising over the mountains. Deputy O'Brien fell into step beside James, and I walked on his other side, my mind churning through everything we'd learned.

"Well," James said once we were out of earshot, "if this does turn out to be more than an accident, we have several people who might warrant further investigation."

"The young woman who was pursuing Mr. Serpentine." Deputy O'Brien counted on her fingers. "The fiancé who was publicly humiliated. And that pianist—Frank—he seemed extremely nervous."

"Frank looks as if he's always been high-strung," I thought of his quivering hands. "And Joey apparently treated him quite poorly. Norman mentioned Frank nearly quit the band in Spokane."

"Speaking of quitting," I said, "Joey mentioned he'd like to stop touring, maybe settle down in Timber Coulee and open a jazz club. That idea, though merely speculative, seemed to rattle the other band members."

"Understandably so," Deputy O'Brien said. "Their livelihoods would be affected by such a move. They seemed to think Mr. Serpentine wasn't taking their opinions into consideration."

"His proposal might have bothered someone else, too," I said. "Ezra Coldwell. A new jazz club run by the magnetic Mr. Serpentine would surely draw away the core customers of Ezra's dance studio and Fortnightly dances—the young people—and potentially put him out of business."

The deputy flipped through her notes. "Was this Ezra Coldwell present at your dinner party?"

"No."

"So how would he know about Mr. Serpentine's allergy?"

"I don't know," I admitted as my suggestion evaporated like mist. "I was just thinking of people who might have some motive to harm Joey."

"You're right about the band members, though," Deputy O'Brien agreed. "Professional resentment can be a powerful motive. Especially when combined with constant criticism and humiliation."

"But only if we confirm this wasn't simply a tragic accident," James reminded us. "Until we get those lab results back, we're getting ahead of ourselves."

"Of course," Deputy O'Brien said. "Though I must say, Sheriff, the fact that someone might have had both motive and opportunity is... concerning."

"Which is why we need those test results as soon as possible," James said. "The sooner we know whether the original dessert contained anise, the sooner we'll know if we're dealing with an accident or something more deliberate."

We walked in silence for a moment, and I found myself thinking about Frank's obvious fear, Vivian's desperate infatuation, and Clarence's public humiliation. Any of them could have had reason to wish Joey harm—if we were indeed looking at something other than a terrible accident.

"There's something that bothers me," I said. "If someone did add anise to Joey's dessert deliberately, why use the one thing everyone knew he was allergic to? It seems almost... too obvious."

"Because they wanted to ensure the result," James said. "Or because they assumed it would look like an accident—someone accidentally mixing up spices, perhaps."

"Or," Deputy O'Brien added, "because they wanted someone else to be blamed. Using anise after such a public discussion about the allergy—if this was deliberate, it could have been designed to cast suspicion on Mrs. Mulroney."

The thought sent a chill through me. If Deputy O'Brien was right, then someone hadn't just caused Joey's death—they'd tried to frame my sister for it.

"I need to talk to Vivian," I said. "Tomorrow, if possible. I want to hear her account of what happened."

"We'll need to interview her as well," James said. "But Amanda—" He stopped walking and faced me, his brown eyes serious. "If this does turn out to be deliberate, please be careful. Don't put yourself at risk trying to investigate on your own."

"My sister's reputation is at stake," I replied. "I can't just stand by and do nothing."

Deputy O'Brien watched us with interest, a slight smile playing at the corners of her mouth. "Miss Parrish clearly has sharp instincts."

There was something in her tone—approval mixed with something else, something that made me self-conscious about James's protective concern for me.

"Yes, well." James cleared his throat. "Amanda has helped with investigations before. She notices details others miss."

"I can see that." Deputy O'Brien's smile widened. "Perhaps we should coordinate our efforts, Miss Parrish, once we know more. An extra perspective can be valuable."

What should I make of Deputy O'Brien's friendliness? Part of me appreciated her professionalism and intelligence. But another part—a part I wasn't proud of—remained uneasy about how naturally she fit into James's world, how easily they worked together, how her hand had rested on his arm several times during our walk.

"I'd be happy to help however I can," I said.

"Good." Deputy O'Brien consulted her notes. "Assuming this does become a formal investigation, I can interview the theater staff and anyone else who might have been backstage." She glanced at James. "Or would you prefer I start with Miss Ashford and Mr. Butterworth?"

"Start at the theater. That makes sense," James agreed. "Amanda, would you be willing to come with me when I speak to Clarence? He might be more comfortable with you there."

"Of course." I was grateful for the inclusion even as I wondered about the easy way Deputy O'Brien had divided up the investigative tasks.

We reached the sheriff's office, and Deputy O'Brien excused herself to go inside while James walked me to his automobile.

"What did you think?" He pulled away from the curb. "About the interviews?"

"Frank seemed terrified," I said. "Whether from grief or guilt or simply fear of authority, I couldn't tell. But he was clearly harboring strong feelings about Joey."

"I noticed that too. Though fear doesn't necessarily indicate guilt. Some people simply become nervous when questioned by law enforcement."

"True. But combined with what Norman said about him nearly quitting the band, and the way Joey apparently treated him—it paints a picture of someone who might have had reason to resent his bandleader."

"If," James emphasized, "this turns out to be anything other than an accident. We can't lose sight of that. Until those lab results come back, we're simply gathering information about a man's final hours."

He was right, of course. But something about the whole situation felt wrong—the convenient presence of a known allergen, the public discussion of Joey's vulnerability, the number of people who might have wished him harm.

"I'll know more tomorrow after Maggie returns from Spokane," James said as he pulled up in front of my house.

"Maggie?" I repeated before I could stop myself.

"Deputy O'Brien." James looked at me curiously. "Is something wrong?"

"No, nothing," I lied. Something was wrong, but I would have felt very foolish speaking it out loud. I'd never been the jealous type. Until now. "I'll see you tomorrow when we speak to Clarence."

"Amanda—" James caught my hand as I reached for the door handle. "Are you sure you're all right? You seem troubled."

I looked at his honest, concerned face, and felt a wave of affection mixed with confusion. How could I explain that seeing his natural rapport with Deputy O'Brien—with Maggie—had unsettled something in me I didn't fully understand?

"I'm fine." I managed a smile. "Just worried about Kathleen, about what all this might mean for her. And for Clarence."

He gave my hand a gentle squeeze. "We'll get to the truth, whatever it is. I promise you that."

After he left, I stood in my darkened parlor, watching through the window as he drove back toward town. Somewhere in Timber Coulee, Joey Serpentine's death was being mourned—or perhaps celebrated. And somewhere else, Vivian Ashford was probably crying into her pillow, heartbroken and alone.

Tomorrow would bring lab results, more questions, and—if we were fortunate—some answers. But tonight, all I could do was worry about my sister, wonder about Deputy O'Brien's easy partnership with James, and try to make sense of a world where beautiful music and sudden death could exist side by side.

Moxie rubbed against my ankles, purring, and I reached down to scratch behind his ears. At least someone in this house wasn't troubled by complications and jealousies and possible murder investigations.

"What do you think, Moxie? Was it an accident, or did someone want Joey Serpentine dead?"

But my cat, wise creature that he was, kept his opinions to himself.

Chapter Ten

Monday morning dawned gray and drizzly, the kind of weather that matched my unsettled mood. I'd spent a restless night turning over the events of the previous day, my mind cycling through images of Joey's golden trumpet, Vivian's tear-stained face, Frank's mild tremor, and Deputy O'Brien's confident smile.

Kathleen was already in the kitchen when I came downstairs, mixing batter with a practiced arm. Molly sat at the table, still in her bathrobe, looking pale and tired.

"'Morning." I poured myself a cup of coffee from the pot on the stove.

Kathleen didn't look up. "I'm making pancakes. Nobody's going to say I let my family go hungry while we wait to see if I'm going to be arrested for murder."

"You're not going to be arrested," I reassured her. "James is getting the dessert tested, and it will prove you didn't put anise in it."

"And if someone else did?" Molly asked. "What then?"

"Then we find out who." I sat down beside her. "And why."

Moxie jumped onto my lap, purring, and I stroked his orange fur. The cat had an uncanny ability to sense when I needed comfort.

"I barely slept," Molly admitted. "I kept thinking about Clarence, about how he was backstage, how he had access to the dessert. What if people think—"

"We won't let that happen," I interrupted. "Clarence is innocent, and so is your mother. We just need to prove it."

"By finding the real culprit. If there is one." The hot griddle sizzled as Kathleen ladled batter onto it. Within moments the comforting scent of warm pancakes permeated the room. "Maybe it really was just a terrible accident."

But none of us believed that. Not in our hearts.

After breakfast, I gathered my things to head to the shop. Molly remained at the table, making no move to get dressed.

"Aren't you coming?" I asked.

Molly glanced at her mother, then back at me. "I thought I'd stay home today. Mother wanted to continue my homemaking lessons, and with everything that's happened—" She trailed off.

I looked between them, understanding dawning. "That's a good idea. What are you planning to work on?"

"Laundry first, I think." Kathleen's voice sounded a bit too bright. "Then baking this afternoon. Cookies, maybe some bread. Keeping busy will help."

"Call me at the shop if you need anything. Anything at all."

Molly nodded and gave me a grateful look. She understood that I understood—this wasn't really about homemaking lessons. This was about a daughter supporting her mother through an impossible situation, and a mother finding comfort in teaching her daughter the skills she'd always wanted to pass along.

The walk to Mountain Melodies was lonely in the drizzle, just me and Moxie, who trotted along with his tail held high despite the damp. When we arrived, Callan was already there, unlocking the front door.

"Morning, Amanda." His Scottish brogue was welcoming. "Thought I'd come in early, what with the weather keeping folks indoors. Might get some repair work done."

"That's thoughtful of you." I followed him inside and shook the rain from my umbrella. "I may need to step out later this afternoon, if you don't mind watching the shop."

"Not at all." He hung his coat on the rack. "Everything all right? Ye look a wee bit troubled."

I hesitated, but Callan would hear about it soon enough. "Joey Serpentine died Saturday night." At his blank look, I added, "The leader of the Midnight Serpents." Silence. "The jazz band that did the concert at the Majestic." More silence. "I take it you were not among those present."

"And have my eardrums blasted out by that noise? Nae, thank ye." He paused. "Though 'tis a shame the man died. Ken ye what happened?"

"It appears to have been an allergic reaction to something he ate."

Callan quirked an eyebrow. "The puddin' yer sister made?"

"How did you—"

"Rose said somethin'. She heard about it last night from a friend who works at the hotel."

"Word travels fast."

He seemed to regret bringing it up. "I'm sorry, lass. That must be difficult for your family."

"It is. Especially since we don't yet know if it was an accident or—" I stopped, not wanting to voice the darker possibility aloud.

Callan nodded. "Well, if there's anything I can do to help, ye only have to ask."

"Thank you. That means a great deal."

The morning dragged by. We had few customers—the rain keeping most people at home—and I was distracted, unable to focus on inventory or bookkeeping. I kept thinking about Joey, about the rest of the band members, about Kathleen and Clarence and Vivian. About how peaceful and untroubled Timber Coulee had seemed only a few days ago.

At around three o'clock, the telephone behind the counter rang, making me jump. I picked it up, expecting a customer inquiry.

"Mountain Melodies, Amanda Parrish speaking."

"Go ahead, please," said the operator's nasal voice.

"Aunt Amanda, it's Molly." Her voice was tense, urgent. "We've been baking all afternoon, and Mother went to get the anise extract for the cookies we're making. It's not in the cupboard. We've searched everywhere—the whole kitchen, the pantry, even the dining room in case it got moved during the dinner party. It's gone."

My stomach dropped. "You're certain?"

"Completely certain. Mother used it Friday night for the torte, and now it's simply not here. If someone took it—"

"I'm coming home. Right now. Keep looking, but don't touch anything else in case—well, just in case."

I hung up and turned to Callan, who was working on a trumpet valve at the repair bench. "I need to go home. Family emergency. Can you—"

"Off you go." He waved toward the door. "I'll mind the shop. Take as long as ye need."

I grabbed my coat and umbrella and hurried out into the rain, my mind racing. If the anise extract was truly missing, it could mean the killer had taken it from my kitchen Friday night—which meant they'd planned ahead, waited for their opportunity, and executed their plan.

Or, it could have merely been misplaced.

When I reached the cottage, Kathleen and Molly were in the kitchen, surrounded by open cupboards and displaced jars and tins. The room looked ransacked.

"We've looked everywhere." Kathleen's wan face showed the toll this was taking on her. "I know I used it Friday night. I remember taking it down from the cupboard, measuring out just a few drops for the torte. And I always—always—put things back where they belong."

"Show me where you put it," I said.

Kathleen led me to the spice cupboard and pointed to a gap. "Right there. It should be right there, to the left of the basil, alphabetically arranged. See? Anise would go first."

I studied the neat row of bottles and tins. Kathleen was meticulous about kitchen organization—everything had its place, and she was fastidious about returning items to their proper locations. It was easy to forget, in the moment, that this was my kitchen, not hers. So she'd alphabetized my spices. What other projects had she taken on to "improve" the way I ran my home?

No matter. I'd worry about that later. For now, I had an anise bottle to find. Or not.

"Could you have moved it somewhere else during the dinner party?" I asked. "In the chaos of cooking for so many people?"

"I've been asking myself that all afternoon." Kathleen sank onto a kitchen chair. "But I can't think where I would have put it. And we've looked in every possible place—and several impossible ones."

"Mother even checked the icebox," Molly added. "And the closet in the parlor, and under the sink, and—everywhere. If it's in this house, we would have found it."

I sat down at the table, thinking. "Who was in the kitchen Friday night? Besides the three of us?"

"Vivian was here most of the evening," Molly said. "Helping with dishes and serving."

"Sal sat here at the table, talking my ear off," Kathleen recalled. "And he came in later to refill his coffee. I think he might have even helped Vivian with the dishes. And Norman and Sweet Lou were out on the back porch for a while. Naturally, they would have crossed through the kitchen as they came and went."

"And James carried dishes in at one point," Molly remembered. "But we know he didn't take the bottle. Oh, this is awful. What should we do?"

"I need to tell James." I rose. "Right away. This seems mighty suspicious."

"But what if I just misplaced it?" Kathleen raised her hands and then let them drop back into her lap. "What if it's somewhere obvious and we've all just overlooked it? I don't want to cause trouble if—"

"Mother." Molly took her hand. "You didn't misplace it. You know you didn't. And if someone took it, Sheriff Holcomb needs to know."

Fear and guilt warred in my sister's expression. "James will understand," I soothed. "And if the bottle was taken on purpose, it means you're innocent. It proves someone else added the anise to Joey's dessert."

"If that's indeed what happened," Molly said. "We won't know that until the lab results come back, right?"

"Which is why I need to tell James about the missing bottle now," I said. "It's an important piece of evidence, either way."

The telephone rang. It was Clarence, wanting to talk to Molly. As she settled in, bringing him up to speed on the latest development, I retrieved my coat and umbrella once more, too anxious to wait until the line was free. The walk to the sheriff's office seemed longer than usual, the rain falling harder now, pounding against my umbrella with all the gusto of a drummer in a jazz band.

The office was warm and dry when I entered. James was at his desk, reviewing papers, while Deputy O'Brien stood near the window, looking out at the rain-soaked street. They both turned as I came in.

"Amanda." James rose and came around the desk. "Is everything all right?"

"I need to tell you something." I closed the door behind me. "It's about the anise extract."

Deputy O'Brien moved closer, her expression alert and interested. James gestured to a chair, and I sat, gathering my thoughts.

"The bottle is missing from my kitchen. We've searched the whole house. The anise extract that Kathleen used Friday night to flavor the apple torte—the one Joey couldn't eat because of his allergy—it's just gone."

James and Deputy O'Brien exchanged a significant look.

"When did you discover it was missing?" James pulled out his trusty notebook.

"This afternoon. Molly and Kathleen were baking cookies—keeping busy while they waited for news—and Molly called me at the shop when they couldn't find the bottle. I went home, and we searched together. It's not there."

"Could it have been misplaced during the dinner party?" Deputy O'Brien asked. "Thrown away by accident, perhaps?"

"Kathleen is meticulous about her kitchen supplies." *Even when they're my supplies*, I thought but didn't say. "Everything has its place, and she's fastidious about returning things to their proper locations. We've checked every cupboard, every drawer, even places that don't make logical sense. The bottle isn't in the house."

James made several notes, his expression thoughtful. "Can you describe the bottle? Size, appearance, any distinguishing marks?"

"Oh, golly." I tried to remember. "It's a small brown bottle, maybe three inches tall, with a label that says 'Pure Anise Extract' in my handwriting. There's a red ribbon tied around the neck—I added that to help distinguish it from the vanilla extract, which is in a similar bottle."

"And who had access to your kitchen Friday night?" Deputy O'Brien poised her pen over her notebook.

"Besides Kathleen, Molly, and myself?" I ran through the list as we'd gone through it in my kitchen.

Deputy O'Brien scribbled. "If the bottle was taken on purpose, it suggests premeditation. Someone planning to use it."

"Assuming it was taken and not simply misplaced." James raised a cautious finger, though his expression suggested my theory had merit. "Though given how thoroughly you've searched—"

The telephone on his desk jangled, interrupting him. He picked it up with an apologetic glance at us.

"Sheriff Holcomb speaking." He listened for a moment, his expression growing more serious. "Yes, this is about the Serpentine case. Go ahead."

Deputy O'Brien and I sat in tense silence as James listened, making occasional notes. His face gave away nothing, but his jaw tightened.

"I see. And you're certain of those results? There's no possibility of contamination or error?" Another pause. "Yes, I understand. Thank you for expediting this. I'll need a written report as soon as possible, but this verbal confirmation is sufficient to proceed."

He hung up and looked at us both, his expression grave.

"That was the Spokane lab. They tested the dessert residue Deputy O'Brien delivered this morning. The cobbler that remained in the dish—the dessert that Molly ate Sunday morning—contained no trace of anise whatsoever."

The words seemed to hang in the air. Deputy O'Brien's pen stilled on her notebook.

"Which means that whatever Joey ate was different from what Kathleen made." I looked to James for confirmation.

"It means," James said, his voice heavy with professional gravity, "that someone added anise to Joey Serpentine's portion of the dessert. Combined with the missing bottle from your kitchen, we now have clear evidence of premeditation. This is officially a murder investigation."

A chill swept the room. I wrapped my arms around myself, thinking of Joey's golden trumpet, his brilliant improvisation, his casual arrogance. For all his faults, he hadn't deserved to die choking, terrified, and alone in a hotel room.

"The missing bottle makes complete sense now." Deputy O'Brien's tone was crisp and professional. "The killer took it from Miss Parrish's kitchen Friday night, knowing they would need it. They added it to Mr. Serpentine's dessert sometime Saturday evening."

"Most likely during the second half of the concert," James added. "When the desserts were left unattended backstage and the backstage area was accessible to anyone."

"But they had to know about the allergy first," I said. "Which means the killer was at my dinner party Friday night or learned about it from someone who was there."

James stood and paced, a habit I'd noticed when he was working through a difficult problem. "Let's think about this logically. Who had both knowledge of the allergy and access to the desserts?"

Deputy O'Brien snapped her fingers. "Vivian Ashford. She was in the kitchen Friday night, heard about the allergy, and was seen backstage Saturday evening."

"Clarence Butterworth." Even though it hurt to admit it, it was true. "He was at dinner Friday night and backstage Saturday evening. Though I still can't believe—"

"We have to follow the evidence," James said. "Personal feelings can't interfere with the investigation."

"What about the band members?" Deputy O'Brien asked. "They were all at dinner Friday night and all had access backstage."

"Sal knew about the allergy from childhood," I pointed out. "And he was in my kitchen Friday night. He even admitted to visiting Joey's room Saturday night after the others had gone to bed."

"Frank seemed terrified yesterday." Deputy O'Brien flipped back a few pages in her notebook. "And Norman mentioned he'd nearly quit the band in Spokane. Professional resentment combined with opportunity..."

"Norman himself seemed frustrated with Joey's behavior," I added. "And Sweet Lou mentioned Joey's pattern with women in every town—perhaps one of them resented it."

James stopped pacing and faced us. "We need to interview everyone who was at both locations—the dinner party and the theater. Starting with those who had the strongest apparent motives and the clearest opportunities." He looked at me. "Amanda, I know this is difficult, but I need you to write down everything you remember about Friday night. Who was in your kitchen, when, and for how long. Any conversations about the allergy, any unusual behavior. Every detail matters now."

"I will. Should I do that now?"

"If you have time." James gestured to a small table against the wall. "The sooner we have all the details documented, the better."

Deputy O'Brien pulled out a fresh sheet of paper and a pen and handed them to me. "Take your time. Try to remember the evening in chronological order, from the moment guests arrived until they left."

I took the paper and pen and retreated to the table, closing my eyes to visualize Friday evening. It'd been around six when people started arriving. James came last, around six thirty. We ate picnic-style—people scattered throughout the cottage with their plates...

I wrote for close to half an hour, documenting every detail I could remember. Who stood where, who went into the kitchen and when, snippets of conversation I'd overheard. When I finished, I handed the pages to James.

He scanned through my notes. "This is excellent. Very thorough." He looked up at me. "I'll need to interview Clarence and Vivian as primary persons of interest. Given that Clarence is your niece's fiancé, I thought you might want to be present when I speak with him."

"Yes, absolutely. When?"

"This evening, if possible. After he finishes work at the bank." James glanced at the clock on the wall—it was almost four thirty. "Can you meet me here at six? We'll go to his boarding house together."

"I'll be here."

"As for Miss Ashford," Deputy O'Brien said. "perhaps I should interview her tomorrow morning at Murray's General Store. A woman-to-woman conversation might be less intimidating."

"Good thinking," James agreed. "Though I'd like Amanda present for that as well, if possible. Miss Ashford knows her, trusts her."

"Of course." Though the thought of confronting Vivian churned my stomach. Could that sweet, misguided girl really be a murderer?

James walked me to the door. "Amanda, I know you want to believe the best of people. But someone we know—someone who sat at your table, ate your food, accepted your hospitality—may have murdered a man in cold blood. Please be careful. Don't take any unnecessary risks."

"I won't. But I have to help clear Kathleen's name. And Clarence's. They're both innocent, and I won't let them be blamed for someone else's crime."

He gave my hand a brief squeeze. "I know you won't. See you at six."

The rain had slowed to a drizzle again. I walked back toward the shop, my mind churning through suspects and motives and opportunities. The missing bottle, the lab results, the premeditated nature of the crime—it all painted a picture of someone who had thought this through, who had taken advantage of the dinner party to steal what they needed and the concert chaos to execute their plan.

But who? Vivian, driven by heartbreak and rejection? Clarence, humiliated in front of the entire town? Frank, finally snapping after years of Joey's criticism? Sal, family resentment boiling over? Or someone else we hadn't considered yet—someone whose motive we hadn't yet uncovered?

When I reached Mountain Melodies, Callan was completing a repair on a clarinet, his skilled hands working the mechanism with practiced precision.

"Everythin' sorted at home?" He looked up.

"As much as it can be. Thank you for watching the shop. You can head home now if you'd like—we're not likely to get many more customers today."

"Are ye sure? I dinna mind stayin'."

"I'm sure. I have some bookkeeping to catch up on, and I need to go back out at six anyway."

After Callan left, I telephoned Kathleen with the good news that she was cleared of suspicion.

"The lab results came back," I said without preamble. "There was no anise in the dessert you made, Kathleen. Which means you're off the hook, and someone added it to Joey's portion. This is now a murder investigation."

The relief in her voice was unmistakable, mixed with concern. "So, someone really did take the anise extract. Someone we invited into our home."

"It looks that way, but there are still many questions. By the way, I won't be home for supper. James and I have plans." I didn't elaborate that said plans included interviewing Clarence. No sense in causing more worry before I had to.

After ending the call, I munched on some crackers and cheese left over from lunch, then sat at the counter with the shop's ledger, unable to focus on the numbers. Instead, I replayed the weekend's events in my mind, searching for any detail that might point toward the killer's identity.

Moxie jumped onto the counter and settled beside the ledger, purring. I scratched behind his ears.

"What do you think, Moxie? Who would plan such a careful, cruel murder?"

But he merely blinked his golden eyes at me, silent as a sphinx.

At quarter to six, I closed up the shop and walked through the dark streets to the sheriff's office. The rain had stopped, but the air was chilly and damp.

James waited for me, his coat already on. "Ready?"

"As I'll ever be, though I'm not looking forward to this."

"Neither am I, but it's necessary."

We walked together through the quiet streets toward Clarence's boarding house, neither of us speaking much. The weight of what we were about to do—questioning a good man about a terrible crime—hung heavy between us.

"Amanda," James said as we neared our destination, "I want you to observe Clarence's reactions during the interview. You know him well. If he's hiding something, you might notice it before I do."

"And if he's innocent?"

"Then we'll know that too, and we'll move on to the next suspect."

The boarding house was a tidy two-story building on Maple Street, not far from the bank where Clarence worked. James knocked on the front door, and Mrs. Halvorsen answered, her welcoming smile fading when she saw the serious expressions on our faces.

"Sheriff Holcomb, Miss Parrish. Is everything all right?"

"We need to speak with Clarence Butterworth, if he's available," James said. "Is he in?"

"He is. Just got home from work about twenty minutes ago. Let me fetch him for you."

She returned a moment later with Clarence, who cocked his head like a puzzled owl when he saw us.

"Sheriff? Amanda? What's this about? Is Molly all right?"

"Molly's fine," I assured him.

"We need to ask you some questions about Saturday night," James said. "May we speak privately?"

Clarence's face blanched, but he nodded. "Of course. We can use the parlor—Mrs. Halvorsen keeps it available for residents who need to meet with people."

The parlor was small but comfortable, with a sofa and two armchairs arranged around a low table. James and I sat on the sofa, while Clarence took one of the chairs, his trumpet case—perhaps he had a lesson this evening—sitting nearby.

"Clarence," James began, his voice calm but official, "I'm investigating the death of Joey Serpentine. I need to ask you some questions about your interactions with him Saturday evening."

Clarence adjusted his spectacles, a nervous habit. Understandable. I'd have been nervous too, in his place.

"I—of course. Whatever I can do to help. But I thought—isn't it being ruled an accidental death? An allergic reaction?"

"The circumstances have changed." James kept eye contact with Clarence. "We now have evidence suggesting Mr. Serpentine's death may not have been accidental."

The color drained from Clarence's face. "You mean—someone killed him? On purpose?"

"That's what we're trying to determine," James said. "Can you tell me about your interactions with Mr. Serpentine on Saturday evening? To be more specific, were you backstage at any point during or after the concert?"

Clarence drummed his fingers on his thigh. "Yes. I—I went backstage after the concert. You see, during intermission, I'd challenged Joey to a friendly musical duel. I thought it would be a way to show respect for his artistry, to engage with him as a fellow musician." His voice grew bitter. "I didn't realize he would use it as an opportunity to humiliate me in front of the entire town." He gave his glasses another push. "But of course, you know that. You were there."

"I understand that must have been difficult," James said. "What happened after the duel?"

"I went back to my seat, mortified. Molly tried to comfort me, but I could barely look at her. I'd made a fool of myself in front of my fiancée, in front of everyone." Clarence's jaw tightened. "I was angry, Sheriff. I won't lie about that. Joey didn't just beat me—he crushed me, made sure everyone knew how superior he was."

"And after the concert?" James prompted.

"I—" Clarence drew a shaky breath. "That's when I went backstage. I know how that must look, but I swear I only wanted to make things right. To apologize if I'd offended him, to show that I could be gracious in defeat." He looked at me, his eyes pleading. "Amanda, you were there. You saw. I shook his hand, congratulated him. He even gave me some advice about my playing. It was—it was decent of him, to be honest."

"I was there," I confirmed. "Clarence was very gracious, and Joey responded in kind."

"Did you go near the dessert that Mrs. Mulroney had brought?" James asked. "Did you touch the dishes or handle them in any way?"

"No! I didn't even notice them. My whole focus was on Joey, on trying to salvage some dignity from the situation."

"And after you spoke with Joey?"

"I left. Went back to find Molly, but she and her mother had already gone. So I came back here alone and went to bed. Though I didn't sleep much—I was too angry and embarrassed."

James made notes in his notebook. "Clarence, I need to ask you flat out. Did you add anything to Joey Serpentine's dessert Saturday night?"

"No!" An expression I could only label as horrified came over Clarence. "I would never—Sheriff, I admit I was pretty angry at the fellow. But I would never hurt anyone. The idea that I would deliberately—" He couldn't finish the sentence.

"Can anyone verify your whereabouts after you left the theater?" James asked.

Clarence shook his head, miserable. "I don't think so. Mrs. Halvorsen can confirm what time I came in—it was around eleven thirty, I think—but no one saw me between the theater and here."

James closed his notebook. "Thank you for your cooperation, Clarence. I may have more questions as the investigation continues. Please don't leave town without notifying me first."

"Am I—am I a suspect?" Clarence's voice shook.

"At this point, everyone who was at the theater Saturday night and attended Miss Parrish's dinner party Friday night is a person of interest," James tucked the notebook in his pocket. "That doesn't mean you're guilty of anything. It simply means we need to talk to everyone who had the opportunity."

After we left the boarding house, James took my hand. "Hungry?"

"Starving."

"Luigi's?"

"Perfect."

We walked in silence for a moment before he spoke again.

"What did you think?"

"I think he was telling the truth. He was angry, yes. Humiliated, certainly. But I don't believe he's capable of murder. He couldn't even bring himself to stay angry—he went back to apologize and make peace."

"That's my impression as well. But we can't rule him out. Not yet. I'll send Deputy Peterson to verify his story with Mrs. Halvorsen."

"Who's next?" I asked.

"Tomorrow morning, you and Deputy O'Brien will interview Vivian Ashford. I'll be there too, but I want you two to ask most of the questions."

"What time?"

"Nine o'clock at Murray's General Store. I know you'll try to be discreet—no need to embarrass her in front of her employer."

Over plates of spaghetti, we talked about other things, both of us eager to set the investigation aside, at least for the moment. We lingered over dessert until we were the last patrons. After dinner, James walked me home. When we'd reached my cottage, James paused at the gate and gave me a sweet kiss.

"Get some rest. Tomorrow will be another long day."

"You too. And James? Thank you for including me in this. I know it's irregular."

"You're helping more than you know. Your insights, your observations—they're valuable."

After he'd left, I went inside, where a single lamp burned in the parlor. I'd hoped to speak to Molly, who'd probably heard from Clarence by now about our visit and was no doubt upset. But both she and Kathleen had already gone to bed, so I prepared to so the same. Looking at the moon through my bedroom window, I pondered the day's events.

Somewhere in that dark night, perhaps many miles away by now, a murderer was settling in for the night, maybe congratulating him- or herself on a crime well executed. But mistakes were made—taking the anise bottle, using such an obvious method, underestimating the thoroughness of our investigation.

And tomorrow, we would continue hunting for those mistakes until we brought the truth to light.

Chapter Eleven

Vivian's interview, sure to be grueling, was set for Tuesday. The girl was already heartbroken over Joey's rejection—learning that his death was murder, and that she was a suspect, would devastate her. But first I had to talk to Molly about our interview with her fiance.

Kathleen was in the kitchen again, this time kneading bread dough with methodical precision. Molly sat at the table with a cup of tea, looking haggard. At my "good morning" she shot me an accusing glare.

"Clarence telephoned last night while you were out. Told me you and the sheriff raked him over the coals."

I sighed. "We didn't *rake* him, Molly. All we did was ask him a few questions. He was one of the last people to see Joey alive, except for his bandmates. His statement is important."

My niece crossed her arms. "You could have at least told me you were going to interrogate him. I should have been there."

"*Interrogate* is a strong word." But not an inaccurate one, under the circumstances. "I was planning to tell you when I got home, but you'd already gone to bed. I don't think it would have been helpful for you to be there, anyway."

"He didn't do it. He'd never hurt anyone."

"No one is saying he did." A headache formed behind my eyes. Coffee—that's what I needed. I took a cup from the cupboard. "The sheriff just had some questions, that's all."

"But James *knows* Clarence. They're *friends.*"

"Yes, they are. But as sheriff, James can't let personal friendships get in the way of his work." I filled my cup and inhaled the welcome steam.

"But—"

"All I can say is, try not to worry, sweetie. If Clarence is innocent, we'll clear his name."

"If?" She slammed down her teacup and rose. "How can you say that?"

"Molly, I didn't mean—" but my words had no effect as she flounced up the stairs. I took her place at the table, temples pounding.

"She'll be all right," Kathleen assured me. Her mood had made a considerable improvement since her name had been scratched off the list of possible suspects. "We're all just a little on edge. You're going to interview Vivian this morning?"

I took a sip of coffee, grateful for the change of topic. "Yes. Nine o'clock, at Murray's." I glanced at the wall clock. "I'm not looking forward to it."

"Do you think she could have done it?" Kathleen wiped her hands on a dish towel. "That sweet girl who helped me in the kitchen?"

"I don't know. But she had opportunity—she was in our kitchen Friday night and backstage Saturday night. And she certainly had motive. Joey broke her heart."

"Heartbreak doesn't make someone a murderer."

"No," I agreed. "But it can drive people to desperate acts. Especially young people who haven't learned yet how to cope with rejection."

I finished my coffee and gathered my things. "I'll go straight to the shop after the interview. Callan's opening today, so there's no rush."

The walk to Murray's General Store took me past the Timber Coulee Hotel, and I glanced at the upper windows, wondering which room had been Joey's. Which room had become the scene of his death?

A memory stirred—something James had mentioned during our initial investigation on Sunday. I turned and entered the hotel lobby, where Mr. Cavanaugh was behind the desk, reviewing the morning's receipts.

He looked up with surprise. "Miss Parrish. How can I help you?"

"I have a question about Saturday night."

"You and everyone else." The poor man looked aggrieved.

I ran through a mental checklist of facts James had shared.

"The body was discovered by the ambulance crew. Yes?"

"Yes. At three in the morning."

"Who called for the ambulance?"

"The night clerk, Tommy Morrison. He'd received a call from a very ill-sounding Mr. Serpentine at around two forty-five, begging for an ambulance. He summoned one right away, and it took ten minutes or so to get here."

"I'm sure you've been asked this already, but did you or any of your staff notice anyone unusual coming or going? In particular, anyone visiting the guest rooms?"

His expression grew thoughtful. "Tommy mentioned seeing a woman in a green coat in the lobby Saturday night. Around eleven thirty or so, he said."

My heart sank. "Did he recognize her?"

"He didn't know her name, but he described her—young, brown hair, wearing a green coat. He didn't think she was a registered guest of the hotel." Mr. Cavanaugh gave a delicate cough. "We have a strict policy, of course, forbidding unaccompanied ladies from entering the hotel late at night who are not registered guests. But it seems that policy momentarily slipped young Morrison's mind."

"Don't worry," I told him. "At this point, the sheriff is more concerned about pursuing a murderer than a morals charge. Now, what about this woman struck Tommy as unusual?"

"She seemed upset, he said. Like she'd been crying. He asked if she needed help, but she just shook her head and hurried past him toward the staircase."

"Did he see which floor she went to?"

"No, he had to attend to another guest who was checking in. By the time he looked again, she was gone. He assumed she'd gone upstairs, then didn't think any more about it."

"Did he see her exit the hotel?"

"No. But there was no trace of her by the time the ambulance arrived around three o'clock. At least, she didn't emerge from a room to see what was going on, as most of the other guests did." Mr. Cavanaugh wiped his brow with a handkerchief. "Is this about Mr. Serpentine's death? On behalf of the Timber Coulee Hotel, we wish to express our sincerest—"

"Thank you, Mr. Cavanaugh. You've been very helpful."

I left the hotel with a heavy heart. Vivian had been wearing a green coat at the concert—I remembered seeing it when she'd fled backstage after Joey's final rejection. And now there was a witness placing a woman matching her description at the hotel, near the time when Joey would have eaten the poisoned dessert.

The evidence was mounting, and none of it looked good for Vivian Ashford.

Murray's General Store was already bustling with early morning customers when I arrived just before nine. Vivian, looking pale and drawn, worked behind the counter, measuring out flour for an elderly customer. Dark circles under the girl's eyes suggested she'd slept as poorly as the rest of us.

James and Deputy O'Brien arrived moments after me. The easy way they moved together—Deputy O'Brien's hand resting briefly on James's arm as she said something in a low voice, the way he leaned toward her to hear better, the shared understanding in their expressions as they surveyed the store, twisted something in my chest, something sharp and uncomfortable.

Mr. Murray—a portly man in his fifties with a kind face—came forward immediately.

"Sheriff Holcomb, Deputy O'Brien. Is there a problem?"

"No problem, Mr. Murray," James said. "We just need to speak with Miss Ashford for a few minutes. Official business regarding an incident after the concert on Saturday night."

Mr. Murray's eyebrows rose, but he nodded. "Of course. Vivian, the sheriff needs to speak with you. You can use my office in the back."

Vivian's face turned crimson and her eyes glistened. Her hands trembled as she untied her apron. "I—yes, of course. Right away."

The office was cramped and cluttered and reeked of tobacco. James gestured Vivian to the chair behind the desk while the rest of us arranged ourselves as best we could. Deputy O'Brien perched on a wooden stool, James leaned against a filing cabinet next to her, and I hovered near the door, hoping this interview wouldn't take too long.

"Miss Ashford," Deputy O'Brien began, "thank you for speaking with us. I know this must be difficult."

"It's about Joey, isn't it?" Vivian's voice was barely above a whisper. "About Mr. Serpentine. I heard—people are saying he died from an allergic reaction. That he ate something he shouldn't have."

"That's correct," the deputy said. "We're trying to establish exactly what happened Saturday night. I understand you were at the concert?"

"Yes." Vivian's hands twisted in her lap. "I wouldn't have missed it for the world. Joey—Mr. Serpentine—he was the most talented musician I'd ever heard."

"Had you met him before?" the deputy probed.

Vivian bit her lip and looked at the floor.

"You had, hadn't you?" I prompted. "You met him in Spokane?" Would she trust me enough to tell the whole truth? That was the reason James had asked me to come, wasn't it? I didn't want to let him down.

The girl's cheeks flushed pink. "Yes. In June. I'd gone with my cousin to see them play at the Liberty Theater." Her voice grew softer, almost dreamy. "After the show, I went backstage hoping to get an autograph. There were several people milling about, and this friendly man—Sal, I learned later—started talking to me. Asked where I was from, what I did. He was very kind, very interested. We talked for maybe ten minutes about music and Spokane and how he'd never been to the Falls but wanted to see them."

She twisted her handkerchief between her fingers. "Then Joey came over. He'd just finished putting away his trumpet, and when he saw us talking, he joined in. And it was like the sun coming out from behind clouds. Sal was nice, but Joey was—magnetic. He had this way of looking at you like you were the only person in the room."

"What did you talk about?" Deputy O'Brien glanced up at James as she asked the question, as if checking whether she should continue this line of inquiry. He gave her a subtle nod.

The easy communication between them, the unspoken understanding—*don't be petty,* I chided myself. *Be glad he has an assistant so thorough in her work.*

"Everything," Vivian said. "My job at Murray's, my dream of going to teachers' college, my love of music. He told me I had beautiful eyes—'like amber in sunlight,' he said. Then he asked if I knew any good places to eat in Spokane, said the hotel food was getting tiresome." Her voice trembled. "I suggested this little café near my boarding house. He said, 'Why don't you show me? Tomorrow evening, if you're free.'"

"And you went?" Deputy O'Brien's pen moved across her notebook.

Vivian hesitated and looked at me. "It's all right," I murmured. "Just tell the deputy everything that you remember."

She faced the deputy. "Of course I went. We had dinner at the café, then walked along the river. He told me about growing up in Chicago, about his dreams of opening his own jazz club someday, about how exhausting it was being on the road constantly. He held my hand while we walked." Tears filled her eyes now. "At the end of the evening, he kissed my cheek and said, 'You're special, Vivian. Not like the other girls who just want to be seen with the band. You're genuine.' I remember every word."

"Did you see him again after that?" James sounded impatient, apparently forgetting his plan to leave the questioning to us women.

Vivian shook her head. "They left the next day for their next engagement. But he wrote down the towns where they'd be playing, said if I ever wanted to catch another show, I should come. He said—" Her voice broke. "He said he'd like to see me again."

"So you wrote to him?" Deputy O'Brien asked.

"Three letters," Vivian whispered. "One to Portland, one to Seattle, one to Lewiston. I told him about my days, asked about his travels, said I hoped he was well. I never heard back. I told myself the letters probably didn't reach him—musicians travel so much, mail gets lost. When I heard the Midnight Serpents were coming to Timber Coulee, I thought it was fate. A sign that we were meant to see each other again."

"But when you saw him at the train station—" I prompted.

"He looked right through me." Fresh tears spilled down Vivian's cheeks. "Like I was nobody. A complete stranger. I told myself maybe he just didn't recognize me at first, that once we talked, he'd remember. But at your dinner party, Miss Parrish, when Mrs. Mulroney mentioned Spokane and the Liberty Theater—the very theater where we met—he still didn't remember. Not even my name."

She looked at Deputy O'Brien with something like desperation. "Do you know what that feels like? To have someone tell you you're special, you're different, you're genuine—and then discover you meant so little that they forgot you existed three months later?"

"That must have been very painful," Deputy O'Brien said.

"It was humiliating," Vivian corrected, her voice hardening slightly. "Especially since Sal remembered me perfectly. When I helped in Miss Parrish's kitchen Friday night, Sal came in to refill his coffee and he said, 'Hey, you're the girl from Spokane! From the Liberty Theater, right?' He remembered. But Joey—"

She couldn't finish the sentence.

"Is that why you came to my house Friday night?" I asked. "To be near him?"

Vivian nodded. "Mrs. Mulroney was so nice, letting me help in the kitchen. I could hear Joey laughing in the other room, telling stories. I wanted so badly to be part of that, to be someone he noticed."

"And you heard the conversation about his allergy?" James asked, no doubt eager to move things along.

"Yes." Vivian's face crumpled. "It sounded so frightening—the way he described nearly dying as a child. I remember thinking how terrible it must be, to have something so common be so dangerous. I knew a girl in school who was that way about bee stings. She almost died."

James exchanged a glance with Deputy O'Brien. "Let's go back to Saturday night. You were at the concert."

"Yes. I was in the front row. I wanted Joey to see me, to notice me." Her voice grew bitter. "But he never even looked at me. Not once during the entire performance."

"And at intermission?" Deputy O'Brien asked. "Did you go backstage at all? To the green room, perhaps?"

"I was going to." Vivian looked at me. "But then Miss Parrish stopped me, saying it wouldn't be good to interrupt Joey in the middle of a concert. So I went back to my seat. But then I saw she went back there herself, anyway." Her voice took on a vaguely accusatory tone. "So I waited until the concert was over, then I went backstage."

"What happened?" Though I already knew. I'd witnessed part of it myself.

"They were packing up their equipment. I—I thought if could just get him alone, if I told him how beautiful his playing was, he might finally see me as more than just another face in the crowd."

"And?" Deputy O'Brien prompted.

Vivian looked down at her hands and chipped away at the garish nail polish. "He barely looked at me. Just turned away to talk to someone more important." She was crying openly now. "I tried to say something else, to make him see me, but he just—he just walked away. Like I was invisible. Like I didn't exist."

"That must have made you very angry," Deputy O'Brien said.

"Not angry." Vivian wiped at her tears with shaking hands. "Hurt. Humiliated. I felt like such a fool, standing there with everyone watching, knowing they'd all seen him dismiss me like I was—like I was nobody."

"What did you do after that?" James asked.

Vivian was silent for a long moment, her eyes downcast. "I left. All I could hear was my own thoughts telling me how stupid I'd been."

Deputy O'Brien pressed. "Where did you go?"

"I walked around for a while. I didn't want to go straight home and face a lot of questions from my mother."

"Where did you walk?"

Another long silence. Vivian's hands twisted together so tightly her knuckles went white.

"Vivian," I prodded, "we know a woman matching your description was seen at the hotel Saturday night." James quirked an eyebrow as if to say, *We do?* I gave a subtle nod and continued. "Around eleven thirty or quarter to twelve. Was that you?"

Vivian's head snapped up, her eyes wide with fear. "I—how did you—"

"The night clerk saw you," I said. "A young woman in a green coat, looking upset, heading toward the stairs."

"I wasn't—I didn't—" Vivian stammered, then seemed to collapse in on herself. "Yes. It was me. I walked by the hotel on my way home. I couldn't help it—I knew Joey was staying there, and I just wanted to—I don't know what I wanted. To see if his light was on, maybe. To imagine him thinking about me the way I was thinking about him."

"Did you go inside?" Deputy O'Brien asked.

"I—" Vivian's face flushed deeper red. "Just into the lobby. Just for a moment. I thought maybe if I left him a note, something to explain how I felt—"

"Did you go up to his room?" James asked, his voice still gentle but insistent.

"No!" Vivian's denial was vehement. "I wasn't even sure exactly which room was his, though I thought I overheard somebody say room ten on the second floor. I stood at the bottom of the stairs, trying to work up the courage. But then the clerk asked if I needed help, and I got scared and left. I just—I couldn't do it. I couldn't face another rejection."

"So you never went to the second floor?" James pressed. "Never went near Mr. Serpentine's room?"

"No." Vivian met his gaze directly, her tear-stained face earnest. "I swear. I wanted to, but I couldn't. I was too much of a coward."

Deputy O'Brien consulted her notebook. "Vivian, I need to ask you directly. Did you add anything to the dessert Mrs. Mulroney made for the band?"

"What? No! I would never—" Vivian looked genuinely confused. "Why would I do something like that?"

"Because you were angry at Joey," Deputy O'Brien said. "Because he'd hurt you, rejected you, humiliated you. And you knew about his allergy—you heard the entire conversation Friday night at Miss Parrish's house."

"But I would never—I loved him!" Vivian's voice rose with desperation. "I know it sounds foolish, I know he didn't love me back, but I wouldn't have hurt him. Not for anything in the world."

I believed her. The raw pain in her voice, the genuine confusion at the suggestion—it didn't feel like the reaction of someone who'd committed murder.

"Vivian," I said, "did you see anyone else backstage Saturday night? Anyone who seemed particularly interested in the desserts Mrs. Mulroney had brought?"

Vivian shook her head. "I wasn't paying attention to anything except Joey. I'm sorry. I know that's not helpful, but I was so focused on him, I didn't notice much of anything else."

James closed his notebook. "Thank you for your cooperation, Vivian. We may have more questions as the investigation continues. Please don't leave town without notifying me first."

"Am I—am I in trouble?" Vivian shrank back against the chair.

"We're talking to everyone who was at the concert and had access backstage," James replied. "You're not being charged with anything. But we do need you to be available for further questioning."

After we left the office, Mr. Murray approached with concern. "Is Vivian all right? She's not in any trouble, is she?"

"She's fine, Mr. Murray," James assured him. "Just routine questions. She can return to work."

Outside the store, the three of us stood on the sidewalk, and James turned to Deputy O'Brien and me. "Impressions?"

"She's hiding something," Deputy O'Brien stepped closer to James as a wagon passed on the street, forcing us all to move together on the narrow sidewalk. She didn't step back afterward, remaining in that closer proximity. "The way she evaded telling us about going to the hotel—I don't think we're getting the whole truth."

"I agree she's not telling us everything," I forced myself to focus on the case rather than the way Deputy O'Brien's shoulder brushed against James's coat. "But I'm not sure what she's hiding is guilt over murder. It might simply be embarrassment over how far she was willing to go in her pursuit of Joey."

"Or it might be that she did go up to his room," Deputy O'Brien countered, looking up to James for confirmation. "And she added the anise to his dessert in a moment of passion and anger. Then she realized what she'd done, and she fled in fear."

"Or sneaked out the back way." James rubbed his temples as if a headache was coming on. "We need more evidence. The night clerk's testimony places her at the hotel but not definitively on the second floor or in Joey's room. He didn't see her leave. And her being in Amanda's kitchen Friday night gives her opportunity to take the anise extract, but that also applies to several other people."

"What about the band members?" I asked. "Have you interviewed them further?"

"Not yet. That's next on my list." James looked at his pocket watch. "Deputy O'Brien, can you start with Frank Dobrowski? He seemed the most nervous during our initial interview. See if you can find out more about his relationship with Joey."

"Of course, Sheriff." Deputy O'Brien consulted her notebook then smiled at James with that same easy familiarity. "Should I meet you back at the office afterward? We can compare notes before interviewing the others."

"That would be perfect." The way James said it—the warmth in his voice, the appreciation in his expression—made me feel like an outsider looking in on something I wasn't part of.

"I'll head over to the hotel."

After she left, James and I stood in uncomfortable silence for a moment.

"You don't think it was Vivian, do you?" he asked.

"I don't know. She had motive and opportunity. But something about it doesn't feel right. The planning required to take that bottle, to add the anise at just the right moment—it doesn't match the impulsive, emotional girl we just interviewed."

"People can surprise us," James said. "I've seen crimes of passion committed by people who seemed incapable of violence."

"I know. But—" I broke off, not sure how to articulate my unease.

"But you don't want to believe someone so young could be capable of murder," James finished. "I understand. Neither do I. But we have to follow the evidence, wherever it leads."

"You and Deputy O'Brien work very well together." The words escaped before I could stop them.

James looked at me with surprise. "Maggie's an excellent deputy. She's been invaluable to the investigation."

Maggie. The informal use of her first name shouldn't have bothered me, but it did.

"Yes, I can see that." I forced a smile. "Well, I should get to the shop. I've been gone all morning. Who knows what tuba-related emergencies might have erupted in my absence?"

"Amanda—" James reached for my arm, but I was already turning away.

"I'll see you later. Let me know if you need anything else."

I walked back to Mountain Melodies alone, my mind churning through everything we'd learned, but unable to fully focus because my thoughts kept drifting back to the way Deputy O'Brien had looked at James, the way they'd communicated without words, the easy partnership they shared.

Focus, Amanda. Vivian at the hotel, hesitating at the stairs. Vivian in my kitchen, hearing about Joey's allergy. Vivian heartbroken and humiliated, desperate for attention from a man who'd barely remembered her name.

Was it enough? Could heartbreak and rejection really drive someone to murder?

***

I was reviewing my notes at the kitchen table on Wednesday morning when frantic knocking interrupted my concentration. Through the window, I spotted Frank Dobrowski on the porch, his face flushed.

"Miss Parrish!" he called through the door. "I'm so sorry to bother you, but I've had a mishap. I'm due at the sheriff's office in thirty minutes, and I don't know what to do."

I opened the door.

The pianist clutched his white dress shirt with an enormous coffee stain blooming across the front.

"I was eating breakfast at this hash house, and someone bumped my table. This is—was—my only clean shirt. I have an interview with Deputy O'Brien this morning. It's important to come in looking presentable and—" He was nearly hyperventilating.

"Frank, breathe." I guided him inside. "Let me see."

Kathleen emerged from the parlor, took one look at the situation, and her eyes lit up with the particular gleam that meant she'd spotted a teachable moment.

"Molly!" she called upstairs. "Come down here. We have an emergency lesson."

"Mother, I'm working on my dress—"

"This won't wait. A wife must know how to handle clothing emergencies."

Molly appeared at the top of the stairs, needle and thread still in hand, wearing a look of strained resignation. But when she saw Frank's panicked expression, her annoyance softened.

"Coffee stain?" She descended the stairs. "That's manageable."

"Give me your coat." Kathleen thrust her hand out. As he handed it over, she sniffed. "Another pipe smoker, I see."

"Not me," Frank said. "But Sal and Sweet Lou both smoke up a storm. There's no escaping the smell."

"I kind of like it," Molly said. "It smells like... autumn."

"Next, we need to get that shirt off you," Kathleen announced with the authority of a battlefield general. "You can't treat it properly while you're wearing it."

Frank's face turned scarlet. "I—that is—I don't have—"

"Oh, for heaven's sake." Kathleen grabbed a large scarf off the coat rack and thrust it at him. "Go into the parlor and drape this around your shoulders. We're all adults here."

Frank fled to the parlor, and moments later emerged clutching the scarf around his thin shoulders like a shawl, his undershirt visible beneath. He looked thoroughly miserable.

"Now then." Kathleen took the stained shirt and held it up to the light. "Molly, what's the first rule about stains?"

"Treat them immediately before they set," Molly recited like a dutiful pupil.

"Exactly. Coffee is particularly stubborn. We'll need cold water first—never hot, that might set the stain—then white vinegar, then we'll see about pressing."

Frank settled gingerly onto the edge of a kitchen chair, his hands fidgeting. Without his jacket and proper shirt, he looked younger, more vulnerable. The scarf kept slipping, and he'd yank it back up with jerky movements.

"Frank," I leaned against the counter where I could observe him, "you must do a lot of your own laundry, traveling as much as you do."

"Some. Hello, kitty." Clutching the scarf with one hand, he petted Moxie with the other. The cat had jumped into his lap and was trying to rub his face against Frank's skinny chest. "Hotels usually have laundry service, but it's expensive. I try to manage what I can."

"Your mother didn't teach you?" Molly dabbed at the stain with a cloth soaked in cold water.

"My mother died when I was twelve." His voice was flat. "After that, it was just me and my father, and he—well, he wasn't much for domestic instruction."

"I'm sorry," Molly said.

Frank shrugged. "You learn to manage. Hotels, boarding houses—you figure it out." The scarf slipped again and he nudged Moxie to the floor.

A boy who'd lost his mother young, learned to fend for himself. How much of his nervousness came from that early loss, that constant need to prove himself capable? I filed this information away.

"How did Joey manage his clothes?" I asked casually. "I noticed his suit was always immaculate."

Frank's expression darkened. "Joey sent everything out. Hotel laundry service, professional pressing. Nothing but the best for Joey."

"Expensive." Kathleen worked vinegar into the fabric.

"He could afford it." The bitterness in Frank's voice was sharp. "Star of the band gets star treatment. The rest of us scrimp and save and make do."

"That must be frustrating." I tried to keep my tone neutral.

"You have no idea." Frank's hands clenched into fists on his knees. "Do you know how much dough Joey spent on that custom trumpet case? Three months' salary. Three months! Meanwhile, I'm wearing shirts until they're practically transparent because I can't afford to replace them."

The scarf slipped entirely off one shoulder, and he snatched it back with such violence that I startled.

"Sorry," he muttered. "This is—I feel ridiculous. Half-naked in your kitchen while you're all—" He gestured helplessly.

"Now, now." Kathleen's voice softened. "Every man needs help sometimes. No shame in that. Molly, see how the stain is lifting? That's the vinegar working."

Molly peered at the fabric. "It's much lighter."

"Good. Now we'll rinse it clean, and then comes the pressing. That's the crucial part—a shirt poorly pressed looks worse than a wrinkled one."

While Kathleen rinsed the shirt at the sink, I caught Frank's eye. "It sounds like there was a lot of resentment in the band. About money, I mean."

"Resentment?" Frank laughed, a harsh sound. "That's putting it mildly. We were all supposed to be equal partners, but Joey acted like he was doing us a favor letting us play with him." He seemed to realize what he was saying and clamped his mouth shut, his face flushing.

Kathleen had set up the ironing board and was heating the iron on the stove. "Molly, remember—you test the heat on a scrap first. Too hot and you'll scorch. Too cool and you won't remove the wrinkles."

I watched Molly test the iron, her movements careful and precise. She'd been fighting these lessons all week, but now, focused on helping Frank, she worked with genuine concentration.

"I never thought I'd need to know this," Molly ran the iron carefully over the shirt's collar. "I assumed Clarence and I would just—I don't know—send things out like Joey did."

"On a music teacher's salary?" Kathleen raised an eyebrow. "You'll be grateful for these skills, mark my words."

Frank watched Molly work, his expression wistful. "My mother used to iron my father's shirts every Sunday evening. She'd hum while she worked. I remember the smell of the starch, the way the steam would rise." His voice grew thick. "I haven't thought about that in years."

The vulnerability of his expression made my heart ache. This wasn't just a nervous young man—this was someone carrying years of loss and loneliness. As if picking up on Frank's feelings, Moxie wound himself affectionately around the young man's shins.

"There." Molly held up the shirt, now stain-free and crisply pressed. "Good as new."

Frank took it reverently, his eyes suspiciously bright. "Thank you. All of you. I—you didn't have to help me."

"Of course we did," Kathleen said firmly. "That's what friends do."

After Frank had dressed and departed for his appointment with James, Kathleen turned to Molly with satisfaction.

"See? That's what these lessons are for. Not just for you to know how to care for Clarence's clothes, but so you can help others in need. A woman who can solve practical problems is worth her weight in gold."

Molly was quiet for a moment. "I suppose I see your point, Mother."

"And," I added, watching Frank's retreating back through the window, "sometimes domestic tasks create opportunities for people to lower their guard. Frank told us more in twenty minutes than James got from him in the first interview."

Kathleen looked pleased. "Well. Perhaps your investigation and my lessons aren't so different after all. Both require patience, observation, and knowing how to make people comfortable enough to reveal themselves."

After Molly left for Mountain Melodies, I poured myself a second cup of coffee and finished reviewing my notes, then followed her to the shop. When I arrived, Callan was still working on the clarinet, and Molly dusted the display of gramophone records.

She looked up at me, her face anxious. "I've been meaning to ask you. How did it go yesterday?"

"How did what go?"

"The interview with Vivian. You haven't said much about it."

"As well as could be expected. There's not much to tell." I hung my coat on a peg and put on my work smock. "Vivian's devastated, as you'd imagine."

"Do they think she did it?" Molly's eyes were round as records.

"She's a suspect. But so is everyone else who was at both the dinner party and the concert."

Callan cleared his throat. "I'll just be workin' in the back room, give ye two some privacy."

After he left, Molly studied me with concern. "You seem distracted. Is it just the case, or is something else bothering you?"

"What? No. I'm just worried about—" I stopped, not sure how to finish the sentence.

"About the case?" Molly pressed. "Or about Deputy O'Brien?"

"Excuse me?" Heat rose in my cheeks. "Deputy O'Brien has nothing to do with—"

"Aunt Amanda." Molly came around the counter and took my hands. "I've seen the way you watch them together. The way she touches his arm. And I've seen the way it bothers you."

"I'm not—" I tried to protest, but Molly cut me off.

"You're in love with James. It's okay to feel jealous. If some girl were after Clarence, you'd better believe I'd have my claws out."

"Really, Molly. Claws out?" The words hit me like a physical blow, unflattering as they were. I wanted to deny them, to think I was above such female pettiness. But standing there with Molly looking at me with such understanding, I couldn't maintain the pretense. I may have been older in years, but when it came to romance, she was the more knowledgeable one, although whether she'd gained that knowledge firsthand or from the pages of *The Smart Set* was unclear.

"I'm not jealous," I continued. "Not exactly. I'm just—she gets to work with him. Share that part of his life. The investigations, the problem-solving, all of it. And I'm always on the outside, watching, only included when it's convenient."

"Fiddlesticks," Molly said. "James values your insights enormously. He wouldn't include you in these interviews if he didn't."

"But Maggie—Deputy O'Brien—she's part of his world in a way I never can be. She wears the badge, has the authority, understands the work in a way I never will." I pulled my hands away and moved to the window, gazing at the street. "And she's young and beautiful and capable. Why wouldn't he be drawn to her?"

"Because he's drawn to you." She came to stand beside me. "I've seen the way James looks at you. The way he lights up when you walk into a room. The way he seeks your opinion, values your thoughts. That man only has eyes for you."

"You can't know that." I turned to face her, surprised by the tightness in my throat. "And even if you're right, I'm not sure I know what to do with it. I've been on my own for forty years, Molly. I run my own business, make my own decisions, answer to no one. What if I'm simply not cut out for—" I gestured helplessly. "For all of this? Romance, partnership, whatever you want to call it. What if letting myself fall in love means losing everything I've built?"

"Or," she said, "what if it means gaining something you didn't know you needed?"

I wanted to believe her. But the fear sat heavy in my chest—not just fear of losing James to someone younger and more suitable, but fear of what it would mean if I didn't lose him. If he truly wanted me, and I had to figure out how to be both Amanda Parrish, independent businesswoman, and someone's—what? Sweetheart? Partner? Wife? The very thought made my feel seasick.

"Deputy O'Brien might be his colleague," Molly continued, her arm around my shoulders, "but you're the one who has his heart. The question is, are you brave enough to accept it?"

That was the question, wasn't it? And I still didn't know the answer.

The bell above the door chimed, and we both turned to greet the customer. Molly squeezed my shoulders once more before helping him, leaving me to wrestle with my conflicting emotions.

Was Molly right? Did James truly care for me in the way she suggested? And if he did, why did watching him work with Deputy O'Brien create such a sharp ache in my chest?

Chapter Twelve

I stood behind the counter, ostensibly reviewing inventory, but my mind was elsewhere—replaying every detail of the investigation so far, searching for the pattern that would make everything click into place.

Wednesday afternoons were typically quiet, and today was no exception. The inclement weather kept most customers at home, leaving me with plenty of time to think. Too much time, perhaps.

Callan was in the back room working on a tuba repair, the occasional metallic clink punctuating the silence. Molly had left an hour earlier with Kathleen for what they were calling another "homemaking lesson"—today's topic was selecting quality produce at the market—though I suspected the real purpose was to keep both of them occupied and distracted from the murder investigation that still cast its shadow over our family.

Before she left, Molly had been anxious, her usual cheerfulness dimmed by worry.

"They still haven't arrested anyone," she'd said, twisting her handkerchief between her fingers. "Which means Clarence is still under suspicion, isn't he? Even if they're not saying it directly."

"James is following every lead," I'd assured her. "He won't arrest anyone until he's certain he has the right person."

"But what if he never finds enough evidence? What if this just hangs over Clarence forever—the cloud of suspicion, people whispering, wondering?" Her eyes had been bright with unshed tears. "How can we get married, start our life together, with people thinking he might be a murderer?"

I'd had no good answer for her then, and I had none now as I stood alone in the quiet shop. But I was more convinced than ever that we were close to solving this puzzle. The pieces were there—we just needed to see how they fit together.

I tried to focus on work—ordering new stock, helping a customer, updating the ledger—but my mind kept drifting back to Vivian's tear-stained face and Deputy O'Brien's confident competence.

Shortly before five, James appeared at the shop door. He wore a troubled expression, and my stomach clenched.

"What's happened?" I asked.

"Can we talk? Privately?"

"We're alone here. Other than Callan, and he can't hear us from the back room."

"Deputy O'Brien interviewed Frank Dobrowski," James said. "He broke down, admitted he'd been planning to quit the band after the Timber Coulee performance. Said he couldn't take Joey's constant criticism anymore, that it was destroying his confidence and his love of music."

"That gives him strong motive."

"Yes. But he also has an alibi—he was playing piano in the hotel lobby from around eleven thirty until past midnight. Mr. Cavanaugh heard him, and two other guests saw him there. There's no evidence he visited Joey's room, much less tampered with the dessert."

A confusing mixture of relief and frustration bubbled through me. "So we can rule him out?"

"Unless he had an accomplice, which seems unlikely." James ran a hand through his hair. "We're running out of obvious suspects. Clarence has a weak alibi but no real motive beyond wounded pride. Vivian had motive and opportunity but claims she never went up to Joey's room. Frank had motive but a solid alibi. The other band members had opportunity but no clear motive that we've uncovered."

"What about Sal?" I asked. "He admitted to being in Joey's room that night."

"I know. But he's family—Joey's cousin. And he seems genuinely grieved by the death." James shook his head. "Though I suppose family resentment can run deep. We'll need to interview him more thoroughly."

"There has to be something we're missing. Some piece of evidence, some connection we haven't made yet."

"And we'll find it." His expression softened. "Amanda, I know this has been difficult for you. Having your family implicated, watching us interrogate people you care about. But you've been invaluable to this investigation. Your insights, your observations—they matter."

"Thank you." That familiar warmth his praise always created came over me. "I just want to find the truth. For Kathleen and Clarence, for Joey, for everyone involved."

"We will. I won't stop until we do."

After he left, I stood at the counter for a long moment, thinking about what Molly had said earlier. About falling in love, about James having eyes only for me, about not letting insecurity cloud my judgment.

Perhaps she was right. Perhaps I was letting my own doubts and fears create problems that didn't actually exist.

Or perhaps I was simply a fool, falling for a man whose heart might already belong to someone younger, more capable, more suited to his world.

Only time would tell which truth would prevail.

I jerked my thoughts back to reality, back to the case at hand. As I made the round of familiar tasks of closing the store, I reviewed the facts.

Joey Serpentine had died from anaphylactic shock caused by ingesting anise, to which he was deathly allergic. The anise had been added to a portion of apple cobbler that my sister had made—cobbler that had tested negative for anise in its original form, meaning someone had deliberately tampered with Joey's portion.

The anise extract bottle from my kitchen was missing, taken sometime during the dinner party Friday night.

Who'd had opportunity to take it? Vivian, who'd spent much of the evening in the kitchen. Sal, who'd come in to refill his coffee. Possibly others who'd passed through, though those two had the clearest access.

Who'd had opportunity to add the anise to Joey's dessert? Anyone who'd been backstage at the theater Saturday night during the second half of the concert, when the desserts sat unattended. That included all the band members, Vivian, Clarence, and potentially dozens of others.

But who'd had both opportunity and motive?

I ran through the list of names in my head for the umpteenth time. Vivian. Clarence. Frank.

Sweet Lou? Like the others, he'd chafed under Joey's arrogant attitude, but he didn't seem capable of murder. But he didn't have a great alibi for the time of Joey's death. Neither did Norman. And then there was Sal, but he'd always seemed so protective of his cousin, even as Joey's behavior clearly irritated him on occasion.

All of them had been in or near my kitchen Friday night. All of them knew of Joey's allergy.

I needed to talk to Tommy Morrison again. The night clerk had always been observant, and he'd been on duty that terrible night. Perhaps there were details he'd noticed but hadn't thought to mention—details that might help us understand exactly what had happened in those crucial hours between Joey eating the dessert and his body being discovered by the ambulance crew.

"Callan," I called toward the back room, "I need to run an errand. Can you mind the shop for a while?"

He emerged, wiping his hands on a cloth. "O' course. Everythin' all right?"

"I hope so. I just need to check on something at the hotel."

"Take yer time. We're no' likely to be busy this afternoon."

The walk to the Timber Coulee Hotel took me through streets already growing dark with the late autumn sunset. Tommy would be starting his evening shift about now. Mr. Cavanaugh typically left the front desk to the night clerk after five o'clock, which might make my questioning easier—one less person listening in, one less set of eyes watching with suspicion.

The hotel lobby was warm and welcoming after the cold street, with a fire crackling in the hearth. But my hopes for a private conversation with Tommy were dashed. Mr. Cavanaugh stood behind the front desk with Tommy, both of them reviewing what looked like reservation cards. The hotel manager looked up as I entered, and his expression was decidedly less welcoming than usual.

"Miss Parrish." His tone was cool. "What can I do for you?"

"Good evening, Mr. Cavanaugh. Tommy." I approached the desk with what I hoped was a disarming smile. "I wanted to ask Tommy a few more questions about Saturday night. Just some small details I'd like to clarify."

Mr. Cavanaugh's expression grew even less friendly. "I believe Tommy has already answered questions from Sheriff Holcomb. And from you. And from Deputy O'Brien. How many times must my staff go through this? It's disruptive to their work, and quite frankly, it's beginning to feel like harassment."

"I assure you, I'm not trying to harass anyone. I'm simply trying to help find the truth about what happened to Mr. Serpentine. Surely you want that too?"

"What I want," Mr. Cavanaugh sniffed, "is for my hotel to stop being associated with a death. Every time someone comes asking questions, it reminds my guests—and potential guests—that a man died here. It's terrible for business."

Tommy shifted uncomfortably beside his employer, his freckled face caught between wanting to help and not wanting to anger his boss.

"I understand your concerns, Mr. Cavanaugh." I kept my voice reasonable. "But a young man is dead, and his killer is still free. Doesn't justice matter more than your hotel's reputation?"

Mr. Cavanaugh's face flushed. "That's easy for you to say. It's not your livelihood at stake. This is the finest hotel in Timber Coulee, and I won't have it turned into some kind of—of morbid curiosity."

"Mr. Cavanaugh," Tommy ventured, "if Miss Parrish just has a few questions, it won't take long. And she's been helpful to the sheriff before, hasn't she? Maybe she'll notice something that solves this quickly, and then it'll all be over."

The hotel manager looked at his clerk with clear annoyance, but some of the rigidity left his posture. "Fine. Ten minutes, Miss Parrish. But I'm staying right here. I want to know exactly what's being said about my hotel."

"That's perfectly acceptable." I would have preferred privacy, but I pulled out my small notebook. "Tommy, can you walk me one more time through what happened Saturday night? From the time the band returned from the concert until the ambulance arrived?"

Tommy glanced at Mr. Cavanaugh, who gave a curt nod of permission, then leaned against the desk. "Well, most of the band members came back around eleven o'clock, maybe a few minutes after. They were in good spirits—you could tell the concert had gone well."

"Do you remember the order they arrived? Who came in when?"

"Mr. Lancaster—Sweet Lou—he came through first with Mr. Dobrowski. Frank, his name is. They were talking about the performance, seemed pleased. They both headed upstairs to the second floor. Then Mr. Walsh—Norman—came in maybe five minutes later. Asked me about breakfast times, then followed the others upstairs."

"No one took the elevator?"

"No. They were all on the second floor, just one flight up. All except Mr. Benedetti, whose room is here on the first floor."

"What time did Mr. Benedetti come in?"

Tommy's eyes flickered toward Mr. Cavanaugh again before answering. "He came through maybe ten minutes after Norman. Seemed in a good mood, friendly like always. Said goodnight and headed toward his room—that's room seven, down that hallway from the lobby." He pointed.

"Did you see him again after that?"

"Yes, maybe fifteen minutes later. He came back through the lobby and went upstairs."

My attention sharpened. "He went upstairs? Do you know why?"

"I assumed he was visiting one of the other band members. Based on past hotel guests, musicians tend to keep odd hours, like to talk about the performance after it's over. He was carrying something, too." He glanced at Mr. Cavanaugh again, as if seeking permission to continue. "Looked like one of those fancy glass dishes the hotel dining room uses to serve ice cream."

The dessert. Sal had taken Joey's dessert to his room.

Mr. Cavanaugh interjected sharply. "None of my staff saw anything improper. The band members were free to visit each other's rooms, and guests often borrow dishes from the dining room. As long as they don't abscond with them in their luggage, there's nothing sinister about that."

"Of course not," I agreed. "Tommy, did you see Sal come back down?"

"Yes, maybe fifteen minutes later. He came down the stairs, nodded to me, and went back toward his room."

"How did he seem? His demeanor?"

Tommy considered this carefully, clearly aware of his employer's scrutiny. "Normal, I'd say. Maybe a little quieter than usual, but not upset or agitated. Just... thoughtful, maybe?"

"What happened after that?"

"Mr. Dobrowski came back down around eleven thirty to play the piano. He said it helps him relax after a performance. Beautiful playing. He stayed until at least midnight, maybe a little after."

"Did you see anyone else moving about the hotel between midnight and when you called for the ambulance?"

Tommy's expression grew troubled. "There was a young woman who came in around midnight. Brown hair, wearing a green coat, looked like she'd been crying. She stood by the stairs for a minute or two, like she was trying to decide whether to go up. I asked if I could help her find someone, but she just shook her head. When I looked again, she was gone."

"That would have been Vivian Ashford."

"After she left, it was quiet for a while," Tommy continued. "Around two, I did my hourly rounds—checking the front door lock, making sure the fire was banked properly. When I walked past the hallway toward the first-floor rooms, I noticed light coming from under the door of room seven. That's Mr. Benedetti's room."

"At two in the morning?" I scribbled a note.

"Yes, ma'am. I just figured he couldn't sleep. Some people have trouble sleeping in hotels."

"Did you hear anything? Any sounds from his room?"

"No, ma'am. It was quiet. Just the light under the door."

"What happened after that?"

Mr. Cavanaugh shifted impatiently. "We've been through all this with the sheriff. Tommy has told this story three times already."

"Please, Mr. Cavanaugh," I said. "This is important. Tommy, what happened after you made your rounds?"

Tommy looked at his employer, who nodded curtly.

"I made myself some coffee in the back office. Around two forty-five, I heard footsteps run upstairs. Quick footsteps, like someone hurrying. Then I heard a door open and close on the second floor."

Mr. Cavanaugh interrupted again. "Hotels have sounds at all hours. Guests getting up for water, using the facilities. It doesn't mean anything nefarious."

I ignored him, keeping my focus on Tommy. "Did you see who it was?"

"No, ma'am. Like I said, I was in the back office. But a few minutes later—maybe two fifty or so—the telephone rang. Someone calling for an ambulance, said there was a medical emergency at the Timber Coulee Hotel, room ten."

"What exactly did the caller say?"

Tommy's face grew more somber. "The man said he was in room ten, that he was having trouble breathing. Said he'd eaten something he was allergic to and needed help right away. The voice was strained, hard to understand—the poor man was clearly in distress—but he gave the room number clearly enough."

"Did the caller tell you his name?"

"No, ma'am. He only said, 'This is room ten. I need an ambulance. I can't breathe. I ate something—' and then he made this gasping sound, and said 'allergic' and 'help' before the line went dead."

"You said the voice was strained and hard to understand. Could you definitively identify it as Mr. Serpentine's voice?"

Tommy hesitated, glancing at Mr. Cavanaugh, who was now watching the conversation with sharp interest. "I—I assumed it was him because the call was coming from room ten. That's what I told the sheriff. But I've been thinking it over. The voice was so strained, so out of breath—I suppose it could have been anyone. I wouldn't swear in court that I recognized Mr. Serpentine's voice specifically."

"How did you know it was room ten? Could you tell from the switch-board?"

"I checked the log later, after Sheriff Holcomb asked. The call came from room ten—Mr. Serpentine's room."

So the call had come from Joey's room. Had that been Joey's final act, his last words begging for help?

"What happened after the call?"

"I immediately telephoned for the ambulance and Dr. Moriarty. They were here within ten minutes. I directed them up to room ten, ran up with them to show them which room it was."

"Was the door locked?"

"No, ma'am. It pushed open when we knocked. And that's when we found Mr. Serpentine." Tommy's voice grew quieter. "He was lying on the floor, dressed in his nightclothes. But he was—he was already gone. Dr. Moriarty checked for a pulse, checked his breathing, but there was nothing to be done. He said Mr. Serpentine had been dead for at least an hour, maybe longer."

At least an hour. Which meant Joey had died around one-thirty or two o'clock—well before the ambulance was called. If so, then who'd called the front desk?

"Who came out of their rooms when the ambulance arrived?"

"Most everyone on the second floor came out to see what the commotion was about. Norman, Sweet Lou, Frank—they all came out in their robes and nightclothes, asking what had happened. They seemed genuinely shocked and confused."

"What about Sal? When did you see him?"

Tommy squinted. "That's what struck me as odd. When I was running up the stairs with the ambulance crew—this was around two fifty-five—I noticed light still coming from under the door of room seven. And when we came back down after—after confirming Mr. Serpentine was deceased—Sal was standing in the hallway outside his room."

"What was he wearing?"

"That's the thing," Tommy said. "He was fully dressed. Pants, shirt, even his shoes. Like he'd been up for a while, not like he'd just been woken by the commotion."

Mr. Cavanaugh interjected. "That's hardly evidence of wrongdoing."

"How did Sal react when you told him what had happened?" I asked, ignoring the hotel manager.

"He looked like he was gonna faint. Grabbed the wall like his legs wouldn't hold him. Started asking how it happened, saying it couldn't be true, that Joey couldn't be dead. He seemed genuinely devastated." Tommy paused. "He asked if he could see Joey, but Dr. Moriarty said no, that it was now a matter for the sheriff to investigate."

"Did Sal say anything else? Anything about when he'd last seen Joey?"

"He kept saying 'I was just with him earlier, he was fine, how could this happen?' Over and over."

"Tommy, you mentioned hearing footsteps on the stairs around two forty-five. Quick footsteps, like someone hurrying. Were they going up to or coming down from the second floor?"

Tommy's brow creased. "They were going up."

"Could they have been Mr. Benedetti's footsteps?"

The clerk's eyes widened as he made the connection. "The timing would be right—the footsteps were just a few minutes before the ambulance call came in. And Mr. Benedetti's room is right at the base of the stairs, so he'd have easy access."

"This is pure speculation," Mr. Cavanaugh said sharply. "You can't accuse a guest based on the sound of footsteps."

"I'm not accusing anyone. I'm simply trying to understand the sequence of events." I turned back to Tommy. "Did you hear footsteps coming back down?"

The clerk shook his head. "Nope. After the call came from room ten, I telephoned the operator, said there was an emergency, then waited by the front door for the ambulance to arrive."

"Well, you've had your ten minutes." Mr. Cavanaugh held up his pocket watch. "In fact, you've had fifteen. I think that's quite enough questioning for one day."

"But—"

"Miss Parrish, I must ask you to leave now. Tommy has work to do, and we've indulged your questions long enough."

"Of course. Thank you both for your time." I closed my notebook, my mind already racing ahead. "You've been very helpful, Tommy."

"I hope it helps you find out what really happened," Tommy said, then cast a nervous glance at his employer. "If it wasn't just a tragic accident, I mean."

Outside the hotel, I stood on the sidewalk for a moment, organizing my thoughts. The picture was becoming clearer, though still not complete.

Sal had taken the dessert to Joey's room around eleven-fifteen. He'd returned to his own room around eleven-thirty. His light had been on at two-thirty—he'd been awake, not sleeping. Around two forty-five, some-one had hurried up the stairs. At two-fifty, a call had come from Joey's room, begging for an ambulance. But Joey had been dead for at least an hour, possibly longer, by the time the ambulance arrived.

Which meant someone else had made that call. Someone who'd been in Joey's room, who'd found him dead or dying.

And that someone had been Sal. It had to have been. Who else would have been awake at that hour and would have had access to Joey's room?

But the clerk said Sal emerged from his own first-floor room when the ambulance came. And he hadn't heard anyone coming back down the stairs. Even so...

I needed to tell James what I was thinking. This was too important to wait.

But as I approached the sheriff's office, I saw through the window a scene that made me stop in my tracks.

James was at his desk, but he wasn't alone. Deputy O'Brien stood beside him, one hand resting casually on his shoulder as she leaned over to look at something on his desk. She was laughing at something, her face animated and warm, her auburn hair catching the lamplight. And James—James was looking up at her with a smile, relaxed in a way I rarely saw during investigations.

They looked comfortable together. Natural.

An unexpected flicker of irritation rose in my chest. Not jealousy, exactly—or at least, I didn't want to call it that. More like... annoyance. At Deputy O'Brien's obvious tactics. At James's apparent obliviousness. At myself, for caring about it at all.

I'd been on my own for this long. Managed my own business. Helped solve murders, even. Maybe I simply wasn't cut out for romance if a little thing like this was going to bother me so much.

I turned away before they could see me, my important discoveries momentarily forgotten. My feet carried me without conscious direction, past the closed shops and quiet houses, until I found myself at the lake.

The water was dark and still, reflecting the first stars beginning to emerge in the clear autumn sky. I wrapped my arms around myself against the cold, feeling equal parts foolish and frustrated.

Was I being ridiculous? Molly had assured me that James cared for me, that Deputy O'Brien was merely a colleague. And here I was, sulking by the lake like some lovesick schoolgirl instead of doing what I did best—solving a murder.

A murder investigation. A young man dead. My sister's reputation still under shadow until we found the real killer. Molly's fiancé still under suspicion, their future happiness hanging in the balance.

Those were the things that mattered. Not my bruised pride about a man who'd never actually promised me anything beyond friendship. Hadn't that kiss suggested something more? Or were the romantic feelings all on my part?

"Amanda?"

James stood a few yards away, his coat collar turned up against the cold wind off the lake. He must have seen me walk past the office and followed me.

"Are you all right? I saw you walk past through the window."

"I'm fine." Then I reconsidered with a wry smile. "Actually, I'm being foolish. I discovered something important about the case and was coming to tell you, but I got distracted."

"Distracted by what?" James came closer.

I debated whether to say anything, then decided honesty was probably the wisest course. "By Deputy O'Brien's hand on your shoulder and the way you and she were laughing. Very... intimately."

James looked genuinely confused. "Maggie and I were just reviewing the interview transcripts from yesterday. She found something amusing in one of the statements."

"I'm sure she did. The question is whether it was actually amusing, or whether you were the amusing part."

"I don't follow."

I studied his face, looking for any sign of disingenuousness. Only honest bewilderment stared back at me. Good grief, the man really didn't see it.

"James." Directness was best. "Deputy O'Brien is attracted to you. The touching, the laughter, the way she finds excuses to lean close—these are not the behaviors of someone who's simply enthusiastic about police work."

He blinked. "You think Deputy O'Brien is... flirting?"

"I think she's made her interest quite clear. To me, at least. Apparently not to you."

"I thought she was just being friendly. Eager to learn. Professional."

I couldn't help it—I laughed. Not cruelly, but with genuine amusement at his complete obliviousness. "James, for a man who can spot a lie from across a room, you are remarkably blind to matters of the heart."

He looked so thoroughly confused that I almost felt sorry for him.

"Are you certain? I haven't noticed anything inappropriate."

"Of course you haven't." My annoyance faded into something closer to fond exasperation. "Men rarely do. But I'm a woman, and I know the difference between professional courtesy and romantic interest. Deputy O'Brien is definitely interested."

James tugged at his collar. "Even if that's true, it doesn't matter. I'm not interested in her that way. She's a colleague. That's all."

"Does she know that? Have you made it clear?"

"I shouldn't have to." Frustration crept into his voice. "We're working a murder investigation. The nature of our professional relationship should be obvious."

"Should be. But apparently isn't." I paused, then added, "Look, I'm not accusing you of encouraging her. I don't think you even realized what was happening. But James—" I met his eyes. "Women notice these things. And right now, your deputy seems to think she has a chance with you."

James was quiet for a moment. When he spoke again, his voice was careful. "If her behavior has been inappropriate, I'll address it. I don't want there to be any confusion about professional boundaries."

"Good." Then, because I couldn't quite help myself, I added, "Though I confess, part of me was tempted to let this play out just to see how long it took you to notice on your own."

A smile tugged at the corner of his mouth. "You're enjoying this."

"A little," I admitted. "It's gratifying to know that even the sharp-eyed Sheriff Holcomb has his blind spots."

"Apparently several of them." James stepped closer. "I also seem to have been blind to the fact that you might have doubts about my—" He paused, as though choosing his words carefully. "About my regard for you."

"I don't have doubts," I said in all honesty. "Or at least, not serious ones. I was just... annoyed. At the situation. At her presumption. At myself, for caring about it when there are more important things to focus on."

"Your feelings aren't unimportant. And for what it's worth, I'm sorry I didn't notice what was happening. I'll be more careful going forward."

"Just don't be too obvious about it. She's still a valuable deputy, and we need her help on this case. I'd rather not create unnecessary drama."

"Agreed." James offered his arm. "Now, shall I walk you home?"

"Yes." I took his arm and felt my equilibrium restored. But instead of heading toward home, we continued strolling along the shoreline, under a canopy of stars.

You mentioned you'd discovered something important?"

"Tommy had some very interesting things to say about Saturday night."

As we walked back through town, my annoyance evaporated. James might be oblivious to romantic overtures, but he was honest and straight-forward—qualities I valued far more than smooth charm. And if Deputy O'Brien wanted to waste her time pursuing a man who wasn't interested, that was her problem, not mine.

We had a murder to solve. Everything else could wait.

"Sal's light was on at two-thirty in the morning," I began. "Tommy noticed it during his rounds. And around two forty-five, someone was moving quickly on the stairs. Then at two-fifty, the ambulance call came from Joey's room—according to the clerk, the caller said he'd eaten something he was allergic to and needed help."

James's expression sharpened. "Yes, I know. Mr. Serpentine was in distress."

"But there's a problem with the timing," I pressed. "Dr. Moriarty estimated that Joey'd been dead for at least an hour by the time the ambulance came. A corpse can't make a phone call."

"Unless Moriarty was mistaken."

"Have you ever known Dr. Moriarty to be mistaken about anything?"

"No," James admitted. "But the clerk swore it was Joey Serpentine on the line."

"Not exactly. The voice was strained and hard to understand. Tommy assumed it was Joey because the call came from Joey's room. But he said he couldn't swear it was actually Joey's voice—it could have been anyone."

"One of the band members?"

I nodded. "I think it was Sal." When James didn't reply, I barreled on.

"It makes sense, doesn't it? He'd been awake, his light was on. Maybe guilt was keeping him from sleeping, or worry about what he'd done. So he went to check on Joey, found him dying or dead, and panicked. Called for help, hoping the ambulance could still save him."

"But why not just say 'This is Sal Benedetti, my cousin needs help'?"

I worked through the logic. "Because, if he admitted he was there, he'd have to explain why. He'd have to answer questions about how Joey came to ingest anise. But if the call came from Joey himself, it would look like Joey had called for help, had tried to save himself. It would look like an accident, just a tragic reaction that happened too quickly for medical help to arrive in time."

"Except that Dr. Moriarty said Joey had been dead for at least an hour when the ambulance arrived," James said. "Which means he died around twelve-thirty or one o'clock—hours before the call came in."

"So maybe Sal planned to check on Joey around two forty-five, expecting to find him suffering from the anise. But instead—"

"Instead, he found Joey unconscious, and called for an ambulance. Or maybe he even realized Joey was already dead. And by calling the ambulance, he was creating a false narrative to cover his tracks." James set his lips in a grim line.

"But that doesn't make sense either," I protested. "If he was trying to cover his tracks, why call for an ambulance at all? Why not just let someone discover the body in the morning? Why draw attention to the exact time of death?"

"Unless he thought the timing would support his innocence somehow. If Joey supposedly called for help himself at two-fifty, and Sal was seen emerging from his own room shortly after, appearing shocked and grief stricken..."

"He'd look like an innocent bystander," I finished. "Just another guest woken by the commotion."

"Except that he was fully dressed at three in the morning," James pointed out. "And his light had been on since at least two-thirty. Those details don't fit the narrative of an innocent man woken by an ambulance."

We stood in silence for a moment, both of us thinking through the implications.

"There's something else," I said. "Sal took the dessert to Joey's room around eleven-fifteen Saturday night. Tommy saw him going upstairs with one of Kathleen's glass dishes. He was gone for about fifteen minutes, then came back down."

"So Sal delivered the dessert directly to Joey. Which means he had complete control over it from the time it was backstage until the time Joey received it. He could have added the anise at any point."

"The anise he took from my kitchen."

"We need to search Sal's room for anything that might be evidence of premeditation," James said.

"And if he did steal my bottle of anise, it might still be in his possession. When will you search?"

"Tomorrow morning. I'll get a warrant tonight for all the band members' rooms. None of them is completely off the hook yet, and I don't want to single Sal out and alert him that he's under particular suspicion. But I'll search his room most thoroughly."

"Should I be there?"

James hesitated. "I don't think that's wise. If Sal is our killer, I don't want him associating you with the investigation too closely. You've already been asking questions at the hotel—if he finds out, if he feels threatened..."

"You think he'd hurt me?"

"I think he may have killed his own cousin," James blurted. "Whether he intended to or not, whether he regrets it or not, he's proven capable of lethal action. I won't put you at risk."

"But you'll tell me what you find?"

"Immediately. Amanda, this is excellent investigative work. Your persistence, your attention to detail, your ability to ask the right questions—it's bringing us closer to the truth."

The praise warmed me, pushing aside the last remnants of my jealousy and doubt. This was what mattered—working together to find justice, to uncover truth, to protect the innocent and hold the guilty accountable.

"We should get you home." James glanced at the dark sky. "It's getting late, and it's cold."

We walked back through the quiet streets together, neither of us speaking much, but the silence between us was comfortable now, companionable. The awkwardness and tension of earlier had dissipated, replaced by something warmer, more solid.

We said our goodbyes at my door. "About what we discussed earlier—about Deputy O'Brien, about my feelings for you—"

"Never mind." My initial reaction to Deputy O'Brien's overly friendly demeanor now felt melodramatic. And I wasn't a melodramatic sort of woman. Usually.

"I meant what I said. All of it. And when this case is over—"

"When this case is over, I'll still be here. And we'll still be...us."

James's face lit up with a smile that transformed his usually serious expression. "Good. That's—that's very good."

After he left, I stood in my darkened parlor for a long moment, my hand pressed against the door he'd just walked through. My emotions were a confused tangle—relief at his reassurances about Deputy O'Brien, warmth at his affection, anxiety about the case that still needed solving.

But underneath it all was a thread of happiness, pure and simple. James cared for me. Not as a useful assistant to his investigations, not as a convenient source of information, but as a woman he wanted to spend time with, to build something real with.

Moxie wound around my ankles, purring loudly, and I reached down to scratch behind his ears.

"Well, Moxie," I murmured, "it seems that all's well with James. Now we just need to catch a killer, and everything will be perfect."

His steady purring was comfort enough as I prepared for bed, my mind already turning over plans for the next day.

Tomorrow, James would search the band members' rooms. Tomorrow, we might find the evidence we needed. Tomorrow, we might finally have the answers that would bring justice for Joey, peace for Kathleen, and freedom for Clarence to marry Molly without the shadow of suspicion hanging over him.

And after that—after the case was solved and the killer brought to justice—James and I would begin a new chapter. One built not on investigations and suspicions, but on trust and affection and the promise of something more.

I fell asleep that night with a smile on my face, despite the grim business that awaited us in the morning.

Chapter Thirteen

Thursday morning brought clear skies and biting cold—the kind of cold that made you question every step outside. The warmth of the shop was comforting. I stood at the window, my breath fogging the glass, my mind not on the weather but on Sal Benedetti.

James would be conducting his room searches this morning. He'd gotten his warrant late last night, and by now he was probably at the hotel, methodically going through the band members' belongings. Looking for evidence. Looking for my missing bottle of anise extract.

An icy breeze fluttered the sheet music as Molly entered with Kathleen, both of them bundled against the cold. Molly's cheeks were pink from the wind, but her expression was troubled.

"We just ran into Deputy Peterson at the bakery," she blurted. "He told us the sheriff is headed for the hotel with a warrant. He's searching the band members' rooms."

"I know," I said. "He told me last night."

Kathleen set down her shopping basket. "Does this mean—is he close to making an arrest?"

"I think so. He's looking for specific evidence."

"Evidence against Clarence?" Molly's voice was tight with worry.

"No." I glanced around the empty shop, then lowered my voice. "I—I can't really say much about it yet. The investigation is still underway. But Clarence looks to be in the clear. According to Deputy Peterson, his landlady stated he came home soon after the concert and didn't leave again until church on Sunday morning."

The shop bell jangled, and we all jumped. It was only a woman looking for sheet music for her daughter's piano lessons. I helped her make her selection, and by the time she left, Molly and Kathleen were preparing to depart as well.

"I'm taking Mother to visit Mildred Abernathy," Molly explained. "Mildred's been feeling under the weather. We thought we'd bring her some of that chicken soup we made."

"That *you* made," Kathleen corrected with a smile. "And did a fine job of it, too."

They left me alone with my thoughts again. The question of motive nagged at me. Sal had seemed genuinely grief-stricken. The way he'd collapsed at the news of Joey's death, the tears, the disbelief—could all of that have been performance?

Or was it genuine grief mixed with guilt? The remorse of someone who'd intended to hurt but not to kill?

The morning crawled past. Callan arrived and worked on repairs in the back room while I minded the counter, my attention constantly drifting to thoughts of the investigation. Around eleven, I needed to do something more active than simply wait for James to finish his search.

After alerting Callan to keep an ear out for customers, I pulled on my coat and walked to the Timber Coulee Hotel.

The lobby was quiet when I entered, with no sign of James or his search. Mr. Cavanaugh stood behind the desk, his expression sour.

"Miss Parrish." His greeting held no welcome at all. If anything, it dropped the temperature of the room ten degrees. "If you're here to ask more questions, I'm afraid I must—"

"In fact, I was hoping to speak with one of the guests." I glued my smile in place, determined to remain pleasant. "Mr. Lancaster, if he's available."

Mr. Cavanaugh's expression suggested this request was only marginally better than another interrogation of his staff. "Room twelve," he snapped. "Second floor."

I found Sweet Lou's room and knocked. After a moment, the trombonist opened the door, his usually jovial face drawn with worry.

"Miss Parrish." His eyebrows shot up. "Is everythin' all right?"

"May I speak with you for a few minutes? I have some questions about Sal."

Sweet Lou glanced down the hallway, then stepped back to let me in. His room was modest but comfortable, with his trombone case propped against the wall and several suits hanging on a portable garment rack. Normally I would have hesitated to enter a man's hotel room alone, but my determination to help James discover the truth made me brave. Besides, I trusted Sweet Lou.

"Sheriff was just here." He gestured for me to take the room's single chair while he sat on the bed. "Tossed everybody's rooms, lookin' for the goods related to Joey's demise."

"Did he find anything in your room?"

"Nothin' to find." He shrugged. "I ain't had nothin' to do with it. The boy could be difficult, but I'd never hurt him."

"I believe you. But I'm trying to understand what happened, and I think Sal might be the key. You've known him for years, haven't you?"

"Since he was twenty-two, fresh out of Chicago. Talented kid—not flashy like Joey, but solid. Reliable."

"What was his relationship with Joey like?"

"Complicated." Sweet Lou rubbed the stubble on his face. "They was family, cousins from the old neighborhood. Sal brought Joey into the band about five years ago. Vouched for him, taught him the ropes. For a while, everythin' was copacetic. Joey respected Sal, looked up to him."

"What changed?"

He shrugged. "Joey got better, Kid had natural talent that just kept developin'. By his third year with us, he was the star. Gettin' the solos, drawin' the crowds. And Joey—well, he wasn't always gracious about it. Started actin' like he was carryin' the band, like the rest of us was just background."

"How did Sal handle that?"

Sweet Lou was quiet for a moment. "On the surface? He was happy for Joey. Proud, even. Always talkin' about his talented cousin, how Joey was goin' places. But underneath?" He shook his head. "I think it hurt. Sal had brought Joey into the band, taught him everything', smoothed over his mistakes in those early years. And then Joey started treatin' him like—like hired help. Like Sal was lucky to be playin' in the same band with the great Joey Serpentine."

"Did they argue about it?"

"Not in front of the band. But there was tension. Little things—Joey would criticize Sal's playin' during rehearsals, suggest he play simpler parts so he didn't 'muddy the sound.' Sal just nodded, never pushed back. But you could see it eatin' at him."

I thought about the Sal I'd observed over the past days—quiet, supportive, deferential. How much resentment had been hiding beneath that placid surface?

"And then there was Portland."

That got my attention. "What about Portland?"

Sweet Lou's expression suggested he was growing even more uncomfortable. "Her name was Mabel. A real looker. Worked at the theater where we had a week-long gig. Sal was dizzy with the dame—brought her candy, took her out to supper once. I think he was workin' up the courage to ask her to write to him after we moved on."

"But Joey got involved?"

"Joey noticed Sal's interest and saw it as a challenge." Sweet Lou's voice held disgust. "Turned on all his charm, dazzled the poor girl. Within a day, she only had eyes for Joey. Sal just—stepped back. Didn't fight for her, didn't say nothin' to Joey about it. Just put up with it."

Another wound, another blow to Sal's pride. His cousin taking not just professional glory but personal happiness as well.

"Did Mabel know about Sal's feelings?"

"I don't think so. Or if she did, she picked Joey anyway. Can't blame her, really—Joey was a smooth talker, real slick. Sal's solid, a square kinda fella. Not the type to sweep a girl off her feet." Sweet Lou sighed. "After Portland, Sal seemed different. He clammed up. The last few months, he's seemed almost—defeated. Like he'd given up on somethin'."

"Given up on what?"

"On competin' with Joey, maybe. On ever steppin' out of his cousin's shadow." Lou paused and took a sip of water. "Then, last summer in Spokane, the same thing happened."

"What do you mean?"

"Déjà vu. We play a three-night gig. This chick shows up, comes to all our shows. Sal likes her, thinks she's sweet. Joey gives her the up-and-down and *bam*! Next thing you know, the chick's draped herself all over Joey. Now, Sal carries a torch for this girl, but she don't mean nothin' to Joey. I mean, that's how the man operates, right? Love 'em and leave 'em. She shows up here in Timber Coulee, all het up to see Joey, and he don't even remember her name. Even at your party, he gives that doll the cold shoulder."

The truth formed a cold lump in my stomach.

"That *doll* has a name. It's Vivian."

"Yeah. That's her. It nearly killed Sal to sit by and watch Joey treat her with such disrespect."

Pieces of the puzzle shifted in my mind. Years of being overshadowed. Of watching his cousin take center stage, take the applause, take the girl. And through it all, Sal had remained loyal, supportive, deferential.

Until he couldn't anymore.

On the other hand, a woman scorned, humiliated, tossed aside like a used tissue.

Maybe we needed to take a closer look at Vivian.

"Lou," I said, "did you notice anything unusual about Sal on Saturday night? After the concert?"

The trombonist thought for a long moment. "He seemed off durin' the concert. Played well, hit all his marks, but there wasn't the usual pepper. And afterward, when we was backstage, he seemed—distracted. Like his mind was somewhere else."

"Did you see him with the dessert?"

"That cobbler your sister made?" Sweet Lou shrugged. "I guess he took some, like everybody else. I was talking with some folks from the audience. Didn't pay attention to what the others was doin' backstage."

"What about later, at the hotel?"

"Came back with Frank around eleven. Went straight to my room, didn't see Sal again until the ambulance came. The siren woke me up and I came out to see what was up. That's when I seen Sal come runnin' up the stairs. Dressed like he's steppin' out, even though it was three in the mornin'. I remember thinkin' that was odd."

"How did he seem when you saw him?"

"Flattened" He delivered the word without hesitation. "Absolutely crushed. White as a sheet, shakin'. When Dr. Moriarty confirmed Joey was dead, Sal just—crumpled. Had to hold onto the wall to stay upright."

Heartfelt grief, then. Or an excellent performance. Or both—grief and guilt intertwined, the horror of what he'd done overwhelming him even as he tried to maintain his innocence.

"Thank you for your honesty." I rose. "I know this must be difficult, talking about your band members this way."

"If Sal did the crime, he gotta do the time." Sweet Lou's voice was hoarse. "But Miss Parrish—I've known that boy for eight years. That he'd kill

Joey—that's horsefeathers, no matter how much he resented the guy. Hurt him, maybe. Teach him a lesson. But murder? Nah."

"Maybe he didn't mean to." I touched Lou's hand. "Maybe he only meant to make Joey sick, to punish him. And it went too far."

Sweet Lou's expression suggested this explanation fit better with the Sal he knew. "That I could believe. Sal's no killer. But pushed too far—I suppose any of us might do somethin' we can't take back."

I left his room with my understanding of the case deepened but my emotions more conflicted. I sensed in my bones that the killer was either Sal or Vivian. This wasn't a story of a cold-blooded killer stalking his victim. This was a tragedy—of resentment built over years, of grievances nursed in silence, of a moment when pain overcame judgment and led to irreversible consequences... or of irrational passion born of a broken heart.

I took my time walking back to Mountain Melodies, mulling over everything I'd learned. Sal had motive—years of being overshadowed, of watching Joey take everything he wanted. Sal had opportunity—access to my kitchen Friday night, access to the desserts Saturday night, the ability to deliver the poisoned dessert directly to Joey's room. And Sal had knowledge—he'd witnessed Joey's childhood reaction to anise, knew exactly how severe the allergy was, knew what would happen if Joey ingested it.

On the other hand, Vivian had motive—scorned and tossed aside after a brief dalliance of some sort. She had opportunity—access to my kitchen, access to the desserts backstage, and she'd been seen at the hotel late Saturday night. And she had knowledge—she'd overheard the conversation about Joey's allergy.

Could Sal and Vivian have teamed up somehow? Worked together to bring about Joey's demise?

But had either of them meant to kill? Or had they only wanted to punish, to humble, to make him feel even a fraction of the pain they had endured?

The rest of the afternoon passed in a blur of customers and routine tasks, but my mind remained focused on the case. As the autumn darkness fell early and Callan left for the day, alone in the shop, I made notes in my journal. I was so absorbed in my notes that I didn't hear the shop door open.

"Amanda."

The voice startled me.

James stood just inside the door, looking grim.

"James? What happened? Did you find the evidence you need?" I led him to the chairs by the stove, where we could be more comfortable.

He pulled out his notebook. "Not quite. Nothing in any of the band members' rooms."

"Did they protest the search?"

"They all cooperated fully. Except Sal, who wasn't there at all. Someone said he'd gone out for a walk."

"Cold day for a walk." I shivered in spite of the stove's warmth.

James shrugged. "He's from Chicago. An icy wind probably feels like home." He consulted his notes. "Anyway, the only suspicious object was a clock. The alarm clock on Sal's bedside table—it was set to ring at two forty-five in the morning."

"Odd. So he planned to wake up at that exact time. That was also the time when Tommy heard someone moving on the stairs, just before the phone call from Joey's room."

"Exactly. And I found something else—a train schedule, with an east-bound departure circled. Sal was planning to leave Timber Coulee tomorrow. Getting out before we could build a case against him."

"Did you arrest him?"

"Not yet. I still don't have solid evidence." James consulted his notes and read them out loud, all the points I already knew about the case.

"And Dr. Moriarty said Joey had been dead for at least an hour," I added. "So he died around one-thirty or two. Which means Sal knew he was dead when he made that phone call."

"Or when *someone* made it," James corrected. "We don't know for sure that Sal was the one who called."

"Who else could it have been?"

"I don't know."

"But it was for sure a male voice?"

"Yes, male. But a prosecutor will want more than circumstantial evidence and logical inference." James slammed down his notebook on his thigh. "I need him to confess. I need him to tell me what happened, in his own words."

"Will he? He's maintained his innocence so far."

"He will if I can show him clear evidence putting him at the scene. He'll know the game is over." James reached over and squeezed my hand. "But for now, how about we grab some dinner? I want to talk to you."

Chapter Fourteen

James suggested dinner at the hotel restaurant—a quiet corner table where we could discuss the case without being overheard. But by the time our meal arrived, we'd exhausted most of the investigative angles and settled into that comfortable space where conversation could wander.

"I owe you an apology." James set down his fork. "About Deputy O'Brien."

"An apology?" I raised an eyebrow. "For what, exactly?"

"For being oblivious." He gave me a rueful smile. "You were right. Once you pointed it out, I started noticing things. The touching, the laughter, the way she'd find excuses to stand closer than necessary. I can't believe I didn't see it before."

"Men rarely do." The poor man had been wearing blinders. "From what I've seen, many of you are remarkably unobservant when it comes to matters of the heart."

"Apparently so." He paused, seeming to gather his thoughts. "I spoke with her. Yesterday, after we finished searching the band members' rooms. I made it clear—gently, I hope—that I'm involved with someone else. That any interest beyond professional collaboration would be inappropriate."

"Are you?" I asked, unable to resist. "Involved with someone?"

James met my eyes, his expression serious despite the hint of amusement there. "I am. Or at least, I'd very much like to be. If she's amenable."

"She might be." Warmth bloomed in my chest. "Depending on the terms, of course."

"Of course." James's smile widened. "I was thinking something along the lines of exclusive interest. Slowly, at a pace comfortable for both parties. Nothing rushed or presumptuous."

"That sounds remarkably civilized." I tapped a finger to my bottom lip. "Almost like a business arrangement."

His dimples deepened. "Would you prefer something less civilized?".

"I prefer honesty. And clarity. Both of which you've just provided admirably."

"Then we're in agreement?"

"We're in agreement." I took a sip of water to clear my head, since my heart was doing a slow roll that was, in fact, a little alarming. "How did Deputy O'Brien take the news?"

"Better than I expected. She was embarrassed, I think, but remained professional. Said she'd misread the situation and apologized for any awkwardness."

"Poor thing." I meant it. "It can't be easy, working in a male-dominated profession and then developing feelings for your superior officer. At least you handled it with kindness."

"I tried." James hesitated a moment. "She asked if the 'someone else' was you. I hope you don't mind, but I confirmed it was."

"I don't mind. It's the truth, after all."

James reached across the table and briefly covered my hand with his—a small gesture, but meaningful. "I'm not a man who rushes into things, Amanda. But I'm also not a man who backs away from what I want. And I want this. Us."

"So do I," I admitted. "Even when it complicates murder investigations."

"Especially when it complicates murder investigations." James smiled. "Though I draw the line at solving crimes purely to have an excuse to see you. That seems excessive."

"And morally questionable."

"That too."

We lingered over coffee until the restaurant staff dimmed the lamps, a hint that even patient small-town establishments had their limits. James walked me home through streets silver with moonlight, our conversation meandering from the mundane to the meaningful in that easy way we'd developed, warmed by our feelings, oblivious to the cold. At my door, he kissed me goodnight—brief but tender, a promise rather than a conclusion. I'd watched him walk away, his figure disappearing into the autumn darkness, before finally going inside to find Moxie sulking on the back of the sofa, clearly affronted by my late return and my failure to bring him any restaurant scraps. Sleep came slowly, my mind replaying the evening's conversation, turning over James's words like coins in my pocket—precious, tangible, real.

I was alone in the shop the next morning. Molly had stayed home to work on her wedding dress—a situation Kathleen was no doubt turning into a lesson on hemming and fine needlework for the soon-to-be homemaker. Callan was out making deliveries.

As I watched the empty street and waited for Callan to return, my thoughts shifted with a great deal of reluctance from my feelings about James to the case at hand. What constituted solid evidence that would point to the killer's identity, and where would we find such a thing?

James had mentioned that the anise bottle would link the cause of death to the means of it, but that seemed like a lost cause. It had likely been thrown into the trash by now, or tossed into the river, or buried somewhere in the woods.

The door blew open, and a gust of cold air startled me from my thoughts. When I looked up, Sal Benedetti pushed the door shut and stamped his feet against the cold.

"Miss Parrish." He offered me a friendly smile. "Hope I'm not too early. Shop's open, right?"

"Of course." I forced my voice to remain calm and professional, though my heart raced. "Come in, please. What can I help you with?"

"I need a new pair of drumsticks." He crossed to the counter, rubbing his hands together. "Snapped one during the concert Saturday night—got a little too enthusiastic on the finale. Thought I'd pick up a replacement since we seem to be stuck in this town for a while."

"Certainly." I moved behind the counter, grateful for the familiar routine to steady my nerves It seemed important to say something sympathetic. "We were all, of course, so devastated to hear about your cousin's—accident. How are you holding up?"

His hands stilled on the counter, and for just a moment, something flickered across his face—pain, perhaps, or exhaustion. Then he looked away, studying the sheet music display with sudden intensity.

"It's been rough." His voice cracked. "Joey and me, we grew up together. Same neighborhood in Chicago, same block even. We were brothers. Well, not really, we were cousins, but he was like a brother to me." He stopped, cleared his throat. "Sorry. I'm not making sense."

My heart swelled, suspicion giving away to pity. "You're making perfect sense," I said. "Grief does that."

"Yeah." He rubbed the back of his neck, still not meeting my eyes. "The worst part is thinking about all the things I should've said to him, you know? All the times I should've—" He broke off again, then seemed to force himself back to the present. "But Joey wouldn't want us moping around. He'd want us to keep playing, keep the music going. That's what we're trying to do."

His tone had taken on an almost desperate edge, as if he were trying to convince himself as much as me. When he finally looked up, his eyes were red-rimmed.

"About the drumsticks, I have several varieties." I was relieved he didn't want to discuss the case. "Do you have a preferred weight and tip style?"

As I pulled out the boxes of drumsticks, Sal shrugged out of his overcoat—a thick wool garment much heavier than the lighter jacket I'd seen him wearing earlier in the week—and draped it over the chair by the stove.

"Mind if I warm up a bit?" he asked. "Had to walk from the hotel, and that wind cuts right through you. Feels like Chicago."

"Not at all. I've got the stove running hot today." I gestured to the chair. "Make yourself comfortable while you look through these options."

It was then that Moxie appeared, emerging from wherever he'd been napping in the back room. The cat took one look at Sal and made a beeline straight for him, purring loudly.

"Oh, not you again," Sal complained with good-natured exasperation as Moxie wound between his legs. "I thought we settled this at the dinner party—I'm not a cat person." He glanced at me. "So this little ghoul haunts the shop as well as your house?"

"Moxie, leave our customer alone." I tried to keep my tone light even as I watched the scene with growing fascination. What was it about Sal that drew the cat so persistently? "He thinks he's the ruler of both places. There's a small window in the stockroom that we keep cracked open a bit, so he can come and go as he pleases." My face heated as I realized how absurd my explanation must have sounded to a person who was not a fan of cats.

But Moxie, as usual, had his own agenda. Ignoring Sal entirely now, he padded over to investigate the heavy overcoat draped on the chair. His whiskers twitched with interest, and he sniffed the coat with obvious enthusiasm, rolling onto his back and patting the wool collar with gentle paws.

"Crazy cat." Sal turned his attention back to the drumsticks. He picked up one pair, testing the weight and balance. "These are good quality. You carry better stock than most music shops in bigger cities."

"Thank you. I try to serve my customers well." I kept one eye on Moxie, who had now begun rubbing his face against the coat's pocket with un-usual fervor. "Have you been to many music shops in your travels?"

"Oh, dozens. We're always needin' somethin'—reeds, valve oil, replace-ment strings." Sal moved to browse the small selection of records I kept near the window. "You know, Joey mentioned he might want to settle down somewhere like Timber Coulee. Open a jazz club or somethin'. Seems like a nice enough town for it."

"Is that something the whole band has been interested in?" The subject had seemed to bring the tension at the dinner party. "Or just Joey?"

Sal's expression tightened almost imperceptibly. "Joey doesn't—didn't— always think about what the rest of us want. He got an idea in his head and assumed we'll all just fall in line." He caught himself and forced a smile. "But that's just how it is when you're the star, I suppose. You get used to callin' the shots."

Behind him, Moxie had become increasingly fixated on the coat. He pawed at the pocket now, his claws catching in the fabric.

"Moxie, stop that." I rushed around the counter. "You'll damage—"

But it was too late. Moxie's persistent pawing had hooked something in the pocket, and as I reached for him, a small glass bottle tumbled onto the floor.

It didn't break—thank Providence for small mercies—but it rolled across the wooden planks with a series of soft clinks, coming to rest against the leg of the piano bench.

Time slowed to a crawl. I stared at the bottle, recognition flooding through me with the force of a physical blow. The distinctive label. The brown glass. The red ribbon. The handwritten notation in my own careful script: "Anise Extract."

My bottle.

Sal who had frozen in place by the record display. Our eyes met, and in that instant, I saw everything—the guilt, the fear, the exhaustion of carrying such a terrible secret.

"That's mine." I reached the bottle. "That's my anise extract. The one that went missing from my kitchen."

For a heartbeat, neither of us moved. Then Sal's expression shifted from shock to something desperate and calculating.

"I can explain." But his body was already tensing, preparing.

"Sal, don't—"

But he lunged for the door, yanking it open with such force that the bell clattered violently against the frame. Cold air rushed in as he bolted onto the street.

"Stop!" I called after him, but he was running now, his coat forgotten, his drumsticks abandoned on the counter.

I ran to the door. Sal raced down Main Street, his figure growing smaller as he headed toward—where? The train station? The river? Did he even have a plan, or was this pure panic?

What were my options. Chase him? I'd never catch him. Call for help? Yes. That was the only sensible choice.

I flew to the counter and picked up the receiver. "Operator?" Silence. I jiggled the hook. "Hello? Hello?" The line was dead. A wire must have gone down in the wind.

I nearly grabbed the anise bottle from the floor, then remembered it was evidence. I slipped into my coat and gloves, retrieved the bottle with a gloved hand, and shoved it in my pocket. After locking the shop door behind me, I hurried toward the sheriff's office, the wind stinging my eyes. My breath came in short gasps, partly from exertion and partly from the adrenaline coursing through me.

James looked up in surprise as I burst through his office door, wind-blown and breathless.

"Amanda? What—"

"It's Sal," I gasped, setting the bottle on his desk. "He did it. He killed Joey. Moxie found the bottle in his coat pocket—my anise extract, the one that went missing. When I confronted him, he ran."

James was on his feet in an instant, his professional demeanor snapping into place. "Which direction?"

"West on Main Street. Toward the train station, I think."

James grabbed his hat and coat, then called out: "O'Brien! Peterson! Get in here!"

The two deputies appeared within seconds, and James issued rapid orders. "Sal Benedetti just fled west on Main from Mountain Melodies Music Shop. He's our prime suspect in the Serpentine murder. Peterson, check the train station. O'Brien, check the roads leading out of town." He spun to face me. "What's he wearing?"

I told him, as best as I could recall. "And he left his coat behind."

"He's on foot, no coat. Can't get far in this cold. I want him found and brought in immediately."

Both deputies nodded and hurried out.

James turned back to me, his expression softening slightly. "Are you all right? Did he threaten you?"

"No, nothing like that. He just—ran. The moment he realized I'd found the bottle, he panicked." I sank into the chair across from his desk, the adrenaline beginning to fade, leaving me shaky. "The look on his face when he saw that bottle. It was like—like he'd been waiting for this moment. Like part of him was almost relieved."

Using a handkerchief, James picked up the bottle and examined it. "Did you handle it?"

"Well, yes, in my kitchen. But not since Sal held it." I showed him my gloves.

"Yes. That's definitely my bottle from my kitchen pantry. Sal must have taken it Friday night during the dinner party."

"And kept it in his coat pocket all week." James shook his head. "Careless. Or perhaps subconsciously he wanted to be caught."

"The weather was mild most of the week. He only put on the heavy overcoat this morning because of the cold. I think he genuinely forgot the bottle was in there."

"This is it, Amanda. This is the evidence we needed. "He stowed the bottle in the evidence locker, then grabbed his jacket and hat. "I need to go. Stay here if you want, or go home—but lock your doors. I'll send word as soon as we have him."

"Be careful."

James paused at the door, met my eyes. "Always am." Then was gone.

I stayed at the station, tense as Moxie in a thunderstorm, waiting for word. The clock on the wall barely moved, no matter how many anxious glances I cast at its placid face. *Should call someone to wait with me? Molly? Heidi?* But my own fears seemed enough to cope with without soothing theirs.

I poured a cup of coffee from the office percolator and brought it to my lips with trembling hands, seeking warmth. One sip convinced me to pour it down the sink. Who knew how long it had been sitting there? I made a fresh pot to help pass the time as I wrestled with my thoughts.

This morning Sal had been just another customer. Now his life would be forever altered. Should I have handled things differently? Tried to calm him down? Not been so bold about confronting him with the evidence?

Forty-five excruciating minutes later, James burst through the door.

"We got him!"

Chapter Fifteen

J ames strode across the room as if to sweep me up in an embrace, then apparently thought better of it. "We got him. Peterson found him hiding in an empty freight car at the train station. He's in custody. Didn't put up any resistance."

"Thank heaven." Lightheaded with relief, I hugged myself against the chill that had seeped into my bones. Moments later, Deputies Peterson and O'Brien entered, gripping a chastened and shivering Sal between them. Seeing me there, he dipped his head, refusing to make eye contact.

"Warm him up," James ordered as they marched the prisoner to the holding cell. "We don't want him coming down with pneumonia before the arraignment."

I turned to James. "What happens now?"

"Now we talk to him."

"Will he confess?"

"I think so." He hung his jacket on a coat rack. "The evidence is strong. From what Peterson said, he seems ready to talk."

"I'd like to stay. I need to understand why."

James studied me, then nodded. "Wait here. This may take a while."

I stayed near the coffeepot, listening to the muffled voices from the back where James interviewed Sal. The two deputies emerged, and Deputy Peterson sat at his desk across the room, head down over a stack of paperwork, occasionally scratching his pen across the forms.

Deputy O'Brien glanced at me, then at the coffeepot, and seemed to hesitate for just a moment before crossing the room.

"Coffee?" I stepped to the side. "I just made some fresh."

"Thanks." Deputy O'Brien poured herself a cup, her movements careful and deliberate. For a moment, the only sound was the quiet splash of liquid and Peterson's pen scratching.

She wrapped both hands around the cup, staring down into it. "I owe you an apology. For—well, for making things awkward earlier this week."

"You don't need to—"

"I do, though." She looked up, meeting my eyes. "I misread the situation. Badly. The sheriff made it clear where his affections lie, and I should have seen it myself long before he had to tell me." She paused, a rueful smile touching her lips. "You're a lucky woman, Miss Parrish. He's a good man."

"Yes, he is." I searched for the right words. "And for what it's worth, I think you handled it with a great deal of grace. It couldn't have been an easy conversation."

"No. But it was necessary." She took a sip of coffee. "And I'd rather be friends than—well, than whatever the alternative would have been."

"I'd like that too. Maggie." And I meant every word.

We stood in comfortable silence for a moment, two women who understood that sometimes things simply didn't work out the way one hoped, and that accepting it with dignity was its own kind of strength.

"He talks about you, you know." Maggie's tone was lighter now. "When he thinks no one's paying attention. Says you have a mind like a steel trap and instincts he wishes more law enforcement would develop."

My pulse thrummed in my ears. "Does he really?"

"He does. And he's right." Maggie raised her cup in a small salute. "You practically caught the killer single-handed, after all. Not bad for a music shop owner."

"I had help from a very determined cat."

Maggie laughed—a real laugh, genuine and warm. "So I heard. I'll have to meet this Moxie sometime."

"He'd probably try to steal your badge," I warned.

"Well, then we'll get along just fine."

After a short while, James returned and joined us at the coffeepot.

"He's confessing. To everything."

"Did he say why?" I asked.

"Jealousy. Resentment. Years of feeling invisible while Joey took the glory." James stirred sugar into his coffee. "Claims he didn't mean to kill him—just wanted to make him sick."

"Then he must have miscalculated the extract." Poor Sal. Anger made people do such irrational things.

"Do you believe him?" Maggie asked.

James shrugged. "I do, but it doesn't really matter. Joey's dead either way."

"It matters to Sal," Maggie said. "It's the difference between murder and manslaughter."

I placed my cup in the sink. "What happens next?"

James paused, considering. "I think we need to gather everyone together. The band members, Vivian, your sister, Molly and Clarence. They all deserve to hear the truth, and they deserve to hear it together. This has affected all of them."

"Where would you gather them?"

"The hotel, I think. Tomorrow afternoon at two." He looked at Deputy O'Brien. "Can you help me contact everyone?"

"Of course."

The deputy went to her desk.

I reached for my coat. "What should I tell Molly and Kathleen?"

"Tell them an arrest has been made, and they'll receive the full explanation tomorrow."

"And then?"

"And then we give them the truth. All of it. Why he did it, how he did it, what he was thinking." His hand pressed my shoulder. "You did well, Amanda."

"I keep thinking about something Sweet Lou said. That Sal's a gentle person by nature. That he may have been pushed too far, with too much pain built up."

"That may be true. But pain doesn't excuse murder. It may explain it, but it doesn't excuse it."

"I know." I looked at the little bottle sitting on James's desk, such a small thing to have caused so much devastation. "I just—I can't help feeling sad about all of it. Joey's death, Sal's choices, all those years of resentment building up. The whole thing is just tragic."

"Most murders are." James came to sit beside me. He took my hand, his thumb tracing light circles on my palm. "We like to think of killers as monsters, as fundamentally different from us. But more often than not, they're just people who made terrible choices in terrible moments. That doesn't make what they did any less wrong, but it does make it more—human." He paused. "Thank you, Amanda. For everything. For trusting your instincts, for pursuing the truth, for—" He paused, seeming to search for words. "For being the partner I never knew I needed."

A swooping sensation hit my stomach, like missing the bottom step in the dark. "We make a good team, Sheriff Holcomb."

"The best team, Miss Parrish."

Outside, life in Timber Coulee continued its normal rhythm. I returned to Mountain Melodies to find everything exactly as I'd left it—the door still locked, the "Closed" sign still hanging in the window. Inside, the waning light slanted through the glass. Everything appeared frozen in time.

Sal's heavy wool overcoat still draped, abandoned, on the chair. The drumsticks he'd been considering sat on the counter where he'd set them down, waiting for a purchase that would never be completed. I crossed to the counter and picked up one of the sticks, turning it over in my hands.

Such ordinary objects. Evidence of a life interrupted—a life that would now take a very different path than the one Sal had imagined when he walked through my door that morning.

I set the drumstick down and looked at the coat. Should I take it to James? Or would Sal need it when—if—he was ever released? The questions felt too heavy for the quiet shop.

A soft thump announced Moxie's arrival. He leapt onto the counter with the grace of a creature who knew exactly how clever he was, then sat down and began washing his face with one paw, the very picture of feline satisfaction.

"Yes, yes." I scratched behind his ears. "You're very clever. You found the evidence. You're the hero of the hour."

Moxie's purr rumbled through the silent shop, loud and self-assured. He paused his grooming to look up at me with those knowing eyes, as if to say he'd been aware all along of Sal's guilt and had simply been waiting for the right moment to reveal it.

"Don't let it go to your head. Though I suppose you've earned the right to be smug for a while."

He resumed his washing, clearly having no intention of being anything other than absolutely insufferable about his success.

Chapter Sixteen

All morning long, the news that Joey Serpentine hadn't died of natural causes after all, and that a suspect had been arrested, sped over every Timber Coulee telephone wire faster than Halley's Comet. Customers streamed in and out of my shop all morning, digging for information.

"All I can say is that the sheriff has made an arrest." I repeated like a scratched record. "Check the newspaper. We'll know more soon."

Never was I so glad to close the shop at noon.

The ballroom at the Timber Coulee Hotel had seen better days. Once the crown jewel of the establishment, it now served primarily for wedding receptions and the occasional town meeting. But this afternoon, it hosted a much grimmer gathering.

Mr. Cavanaugh had been surprisingly accommodating when James requested a private space to address everyone connected to Joey Serpentine's death. The hotel manager's relief at finally having the matter resolved outweighed his usual territorial protectiveness.

"Use the ballroom," he'd said, actually unlocking the double doors himself. "Just—please, Sheriff—make this quick and quiet. My guests have endured enough disruption this week."

Now, as I stood near the ballroom's tall windows watching the others file in, I couldn't help but note the irony. This room, designed for celebration and music, would instead witness the revelation of murder.

James stood near the front of the room, his posture radiating quiet authority.

The band members arrived together—Sweet Lou looking somber, Norman uncharacteristically quiet, Frank pale and nervous. They took seats in the chairs that had been arranged in a loose semicircle, their expressions confused and apprehensive.

"Where's Sal?" Sweet Lou glanced around. "He outta be here too."

"I'll address that shortly," James promised.

Vivian Ashford arrived next, escorted by Molly. The poor girl looked like she'd barely slept, her eyes red-rimmed and swollen. She'd been devastated by Joey's death, and I suspected what was coming would hurt her even more. Molly settled beside her, taking her hand in a gesture of support.

Clarence entered with Kathleen, both of them looking apprehensive. My sister caught my eye, and I gave her a small nod of reassurance. This would be difficult, but necessary.

When everyone was seated, Sweet Lou spoke up again, his voice edged with worry. "Sheriff, where is Sal? Ain't seen him since yesterday, and we're supposed to bounce outta here on the night train. Gotta get our gear to the station."

"I'm afraid Mr. Benedetti won't be leaving Timber Coulee today," James said. "In fact, that's precisely what I've called you all here to discuss."

A ripple of confusion passed through the room. Norman and Sweet Lou exchanged puzzled glances. Frank's eyes widened with what looked like dawning comprehension.

"Whaddya mean?" Sweet Lou demanded. "Where is he?"

James took a breath. "Yesterday, evidence came to light that points to Sal Benedetti as the murderer of Joey Serpentine. When confronted with this evidence, Mr. Benedetti fled. My deputies apprehended him, and he spent the night at the sheriff's station."

The silence that followed was absolute. Even the sound of breathing seemed to stop as everyone processed what James had just said.

Then chaos erupted.

"No." Sweet Lou's tone was flat. "That's bunk. Sal wouldn't—he couldn't—"

"There must be some mistake." Norman's face flushed bright red. "Sal loved Joey. They were family!"

Frank said nothing, but his eyes misted behind his spectacles.

"I understand this is shocking." James raised his voice to be heard over the protests. "I need you all to listen. I'm going to explain how we reached this conclusion, and by then, perhaps Mr. Benedetti himself will have the opportunity to address you."

"You locked Sal up?" Sweet Lou was on his feet now, anger and disbelief warring on his face. "Based on what? What proof you got?"

"Please, Mr. Lancaster, sit down and I'll explain."

Sweet Lou sank back into his chair. But his hands were clenched into fists, and his jaw was tight with simmering emotion.

James paced, his hands clasped behind his back, his voice measured and clear. "As you all know, Joey Serpentine died in the early hours of Sunday morning from anaphylactic shock caused by anise poisoning. What began as a tragic accident quickly revealed itself to be murder. Someone with knowledge of Joey's severe allergy deliberately introduced anise into the dessert he consumed sometime late Saturday night or early Sunday morning."

Vivian made a small sound of distress, and Molly put an arm around her shoulders.

"The investigation required us to consider several factors," James continued. "First, who knew about Joey's allergy? Second, who had access to a source of anise in some form? And third, who had the opportunity to poison the dessert either at the concert hall or here at the hotel?"

He faced the assembled group. "Let me address the first question. Joey's allergy was discussed at a dinner party at Miss Parrish's home a week ago Friday. Everyone who attended that dinner heard Joey explicitly state that anise could kill him. He even recounted the childhood incident that nearly took his life."

"We all knew about his allergy," Sweet Lou snapped. "That don't prove nothin'."

"You're correct," James acknowledged. "A laboratory test confirmed that the original dessert that Mrs. Mulroney delivered to the theater did not contain anise, but Mr. Serpentine's portion did. Which is why the second factor was crucial. The extract used to poison Joey was stolen from Miss Parrish's kitchen, likely during or shortly after that dinner party. This narrowed our pool of suspects considerably."

Kathleen looked stricken with guilt, but I gave her a reassuring look.

"The third question was opportunity," James continued. "The dessert prepared by Mrs. Mulroney was delivered by her to the concert hall Saturday evening. It remained in the green room backstage, where multiple people had access to it throughout the evening."

"We were all backstage at one time or another," Norman protested. "Any of us could have tampered with those desserts."

"Precisely," James said. "Which is why we had to look at other evidence. Mr. Butterworth, for instance, had both knowledge of the allergy and opportunity at the concert hall. He was present during the dinner party when Joey's allergy was discussed. He also had a clear motive—professional jealousy and romantic rivalry."

Clarence stiffened in his chair, but James held up a hand.

"However, no one saw Clarence enter Miss Parrish's kitchen. And while he had motive and opportunity, he lacked the specific substance used in this crime. Furthermore, his landlady attested that he returned to his boarding house after the concert and remained there until he left for church the following morning. Therefore, Mr. Butterworth, you are cleared of any suspicion."

The relief that flooded Clarence's face was profound. Molly slid next to him, and some of the tension left his shoulders.

"Our attention then turned to Miss Vivian Ashford," James said.

Vivian's head snapped up, her eyes wide with shock and fear. "No, I didn't—"

"Miss Ashford," James continued, his voice kind but firm, "you were present in the kitchen during the dinner party. You heard about Joey's allergy. You were also seen backstage after the concert. You had expressed strong romantic feelings for Joey, feelings that were not reciprocated. When a woman's affections are rejected, jealousy can be a powerful motive."

"But I loved him!" Vivian cried out, tears streaming down her face. "I would never hurt him! Never!"

"Additionally," James said, "you were seen near the hotel Saturday night, wearing a distinctive green coat. A witness placed you in the lobby shortly after Mr. Serpentine returned to the hotel."

"I was just hoping to see him," Vivian stammered. "To talk to him. But I never went upstairs. I never touched any dessert. I swear it!"

"Miss Ashford's account has been verified," James said. "There's no evidence she tampered with the dessert, nor that she ever accessed the second floor where Joey's room was located. Miss Ashford, you too are cleared of any suspicion."

Vivian's sobs grew into a wail, but whether from relief or continued distress, I couldn't tell.

"Which brought us back to the band members," James continued. "All of you had knowledge of the allergy. All of you were present at the dinner party and had potential access to Miss Parrish's kitchen. All of you had opportunity backstage at the concert hall."

"Horsefeathers," Sweet Lou interjected. "You're sayin' any one of us could have done it. That's not proof, Sheriff. That's speculation."

"You're right," James agreed. "Which is why I obtained a warrant to search all of your hotel rooms. I was looking for specific evidence—the bottle of anise extract that was stolen, any indication of premeditation, any sign of guilt or flight."

Frank shifted uncomfortably.

Norman leaned forward, his expression intent.

James's voice took on a harder edge. "In Mr. Benedetti's room, I found several items of interest. First, his alarm clock was set for two forty-five in the morning—the exact time when the night clerk heard someone moving on the stairs, just minutes before a phone call came from Joey's room requesting urgent medical help."

Sweet Lou's face had taken on an a sickly cast.

"Second, I found a train schedule with one of today's departures circled in pencil. Mr. Benedetti was planning to leave town as quickly as possible—unusual behavior for someone with nothing to hide."

"That's still not proof he killed Joey." But the conviction had leached from Norman's voice. "We were planning to leave tonight. All of us. We're heading to Seattle."

"You're correct," James said. "Except that the departure Mr. Benedetti marked was not headed toward Seattle, but in the opposite direction, toward Minneapolis."

Murmurs sounded all around. "The conclusive proof came yesterday," James continued, "when Miss Parrish discovered the stolen bottle of anise extract hidden in Mr. Benedetti's coat pocket."

He gestured to me, and I held up the brown glass bottle so everyone could see it.

"This bottle, with Miss Parrish's distinctive handwritten label and attached ribbon, went missing from her kitchen pantry on Friday night. Yesterday, it was found in Mr. Benedetti's overcoat—a coat he hadn't worn for several days due to the milder weather earlier this week. When confronted with this evidence, Mr. Benedetti fled."

The room had fallen completely silent. Sweet Lou sat as if carved from stone. Norman looked as if he might lose his breakfast. Frank held his head in his hands.

After what felt like an eternity but was probably only a few minutes, the double doors opened and Deputy O'Brien entered, followed by Deputy Peterson. Between them, hands cuffed, was Sal Benedetti.

His eyes found mine, and they held a mixture of shame, resignation, and something that might have been gratitude. As if being caught was, in some strange way, exactly what he'd needed.

"Salvatore Benedetti," James tone was formal, "you've agreed to address everyone present. Is that still your wish?"

For a moment, there was absolute silence in the room. Then Sal cleared his throat.

"Before anyone says anythin', the sheriff has told me my rights." He addressed the crowd. "And I don't wanna remain silent. I told him every-thing, and now I'll tell you everything. I owe you that much. I'm—I'm tired of sneakin' and runnin'. I just want it to be over."

Sweet Lou spoke up. "I don't believe it. Sal, you wouldn't. You couldn't. Joey was your cousin. You grew up together."

James approached Sal and said something to him. The two conversed for a few minutes, then Sal nodded. James turned back to face the rest of us.

"I know this is difficult to accept," James said. "Which is why I've asked Mr. Benedetti to address you himself. He has requested the opportunity to explain what happened, and I believe you all deserve to hear the truth directly from him."

The reaction was immediate and visceral. Sweet Lou made a sound like he'd been punched. Norman stood, then sat back down, his hands gripping the arms of his chair. Frank looked away, unable to meet Sal's eyes.

Vivian stared at Sal with an expression of complete incomprehension, as if she were looking at a stranger rather than the kind man who'd helped her with dishes at the dinner party.

Sal was led to the center of the room, where he faced his former bandmates, his friends, the people who'd trusted him. His shoulders slumped, his eyes shadowed with exhaustion and something that looked almost like relief.

"Sal." Sweet Lou's single word held a world of pain. "Say it ain't so. Tell 'em you didn't do this."

Sal met his bandmate's eyes, and when he spoke, his voice was barely above a whisper. "I can't tell you that, Lou. Because I did. I killed Joey. I poisoned him with anise extract. It was me."

Chapter Seventeen

Sweet Lou made a sound like a wounded animal. Norman turned away, his hand over his mouth. Tears pooled behind Frank's round lenses.

"Why?" Sweet Lou's voice broke on the word. "For Pete's sake, Sal, why? He was your cousin. Your family. You brought him into this band. You vouched for him. How could you—"

"Because I hated him." The rawness in Sal's voice silenced everyone. "Because I loved him and I hated him in equal measure, and I couldn't stand it anymore. I couldn't stand watchin' him take everythin' I wanted and throw it away like it meant nothin'."

He slid his eyes toward Vivian, and his expression held such anguish that she flinched.

"You," he said. "In Spokane. You came to the show. You laughed at my jokes. You asked me about my music, about where I grew up, about my family. You saw me, Vivian. Not Joey's cousin, not the drummer in the background. You saw *me*."

Vivian shook her head, tears streaming down her face. "I didn't know. I never realized—"

"How could you?" Sal's laugh was bitter. "Joey was the sun, and I was just the shadow he cast. And when he noticed you payin' attention to me, he couldn't stand it. One lousy day. That's all it took for him to make you forget I existed."

"I didn't mean to," Vivian whispered. "I didn't mean to hurt you."

"I know you didn't. And Joey—Joey didn't care about you at all. You were just another conquest to him. Another girl who fell for his charm. He couldn't even remember your name when you showed up here in Timber Coulee." Sal's voice was thick with bitterness. "But I remembered. I remembered everything. A girl in Portland before you, and dozens of other small cruelties before that. Every solo he took that should have been mine. Every bit of applause he soaked up while the rest of us just provided background. Every time he treated me like hired help instead of family."

Sweet Lou stared at Sal as if seeing him for the first time. "So you up and killed him? Because of jealousy? and a girl?"

"I didn't *decide* to kill him." Sal's voice rose with anguish. "I just wanted to make him sick. I wanted him to miss one show, one chance to be the center of attention. I wanted him to feel vulnerable and weak instead of invincible."

"How?" James encouraged. "Tell them how you did it."

Sal took a shuddering breath. "I took the anise extract from Miss Parrish's kitchen. I wasn't sure how I was going to use it—maybe put it in his mornin' coffee or something—but after the concert Saturday night, I saw my opportunity. See, Mrs. Mulroney had brought that cobbler to the green room during intermission, and most of us ate it up, but Joey wanted to save his for later, so she wrapped his dish in waxed paper, real nice, for him to take back to the hotel. It was sittin' on a table in the green room, and nobody was payin' attention. After we packed up our stuff, I saw he'd forgotten his dessert, and he'd already left. So I took it back to my room. That's when I added the anise extract, just a few drops. I thought it would be enough to make him miserable but not—not kill him."

"But it did. It killed him." Norman's tone was hollow.

"I miscalculated," Sal whispered. "Used too much, or his allergy was worse than I remembered from when we were kids, or—I dunno. But I added it, stirred it into that cobbler."

"And then you delivered it to his room," James prompted, compassion in his tone.

Sal nodded. "I told him he forgot it. He was real grateful. Joey was in such a good mood, riding high from the concert. He was talkin' about openin' a jazz club here in Timber Coulee."

"Did you stay and watch him eat it?" Frank demanded.

"No. He said he'd eat it later, and I told him he'd better eat it while it was fresh, or Mrs. Mulroney would find out and haunt him forever." At Kathleen's wounded expression, he added, "It was a joke, you know. Like how you never turn down an Italian nonna's cookin'. Not that you're an Italian nonna, Mrs. Mulroney. Or a ghost, for that matter. No offense."

"None taken." Kathleen said stiffly.

"Anyway, I don't know what time he ate it. Or how long it took for the anise to... you know." His voice wavered.

"We're getting off track here," James prompted. "What happened next?"

"After I said Mrs. Mulroney would haunt him, he laughed and said, "like that chick at the train station." Sal's voice broke as he looked at Vivian again. "He couldn't even remember your name."

Vivian whimpered, and Molly pulled her close.

"That's when I knew I was right to do what I done," Sal continued, his face crumpling. "That's when I stopped feelin' guilty about it. I went back to my room and tried to sleep, but I couldn't. I kept thinking about what would happen, about how long it would take for him to have a reaction, about how sick he'd get. Around midnight, I set my alarm for two forty-five. I told myself I just wanted to check on him, make sure he was all right."

"But he wasn't all right," James prompted.

"When I got to his room, he was already—" Sal's voice failed for a moment. When he spoke again, it was barely audible. "He was on the floor next to the bed, and his face—I could tell right away. He was dead. Dead because of me. Because I wanted to hurt him, and I killed him instead."

The ballroom was silent as a crypt except for the sound of Sal's ragged breathing and Vivian's muffled sobs.

"What did you do then?" James asked.

"I panicked. I thought if I could make it look like Joey had called for help himself, like he'd realized he was in trouble and tried to get the doctor—maybe people would think it was just a tragic accident. So I imitated his voice as best I could and called down to the front desk. Then I went back to my room and waited for the ambulance to arrive."

"You were fully dressed when the ambulance came at three in the morning," James noted. "Several people noticed."

"I didn't even think of puttin' on my nightclothes." Sal looked around at the faces staring at him—shocked, betrayed, heartbroken. "I know it was stupid. I know I was going to get caught eventually. Part of me wanted to confess from the very beginnin'."

"Then why didn't you?" Sweet Lou's voice was thick with tears and rage. "Why put us all through the ringer? Why let us wail and wonder and point fingers at each other?"

"Because I'm a coward," Sal admitted. "Because some part of me kept hopin' I could get away with it. That I could just leave town and pretend it never happened. But the worst part is, I loved Joey like a brother, and I hated him like one too. And now he's dead, and it's my fault, and I will live with that for the rest of my life."

Sweet Lou surged to his feet, his face a mask of grief and fury. "You wrecked this band. You wrecked everything we built together. And for what? Jealousy? Pride? Because Joey was a better musician than you?"

"Because Joey made me feel invisible," Sal shot back, some spark of defiance flaring. "Because every day of my life with this band was a reminder that I would never be good enough, never be special enough, never be anything more than Joey Serpentine's cousin who played drums in the background."

"So you iced him." Sweet Lou's voice was flat, dead. "You iced the most talented trumpeter I've ever known 'cause you couldn't handle being second-best."

"I didn't mean to kill him!" Sal's shout echoed in the ballroom. "I just wanted him to hurt. I wanted him to feel a fraction of what I felt every single day. But I miscalculated, and now—now he's dead, and I have to live with that. Don't you think I'm sufferin'? Don't you think I see his face every time I close my eyes?"

"Good," Sweet Lou said in an icy tone. "I hope you see his face every day for the rest of your life. I hope it haunts you in prison the way it's gonna haunt me out here."

He turned to James. "Are we done here, Sheriff? 'Cause I can't look at him anymore. I can't stand being in the same room with him."

James nodded. "If anyone has questions, now is the time. Otherwise, yes, we're finished here."

"I have a question." Norman's voice shook with anger. "What happens to the band now? We can't exactly tour with our drummer in prison for murdering our lead trumpet player."

The practical concern, so mundane in the face of such tragedy, seemed to shock everyone back to reality.

"I know from nothin'." Sweet Lou sounded exhausted. "I dunno, Norman. Right now, I just wanna blow this godforsaken town and try to figure out what's next."

Frank spoke for the first time, his voice barely audible. "We could stay. Here in Timber Coulee. Open that club Joey was talking about. As a—as a memorial, maybe. So his music doesn't die with him."

Sweet Lou looked at Frank with something like surprise. "You wanna stay here? After all this?"

"I don't want to get on another train and pretend this never happened," Frank murmured. "I don't want to play in another city with Joey's ghost following us. Maybe—maybe we could make something good come out of this tragedy. Maybe we owe him that much."

Norman nodded. "I—I think I'd like that. A club for Joey. Keep his music alive."

Sweet Lou looked at his remaining band members, then at Sal, then back again. "All right," he said finally. "Let's think about it."

Sal was sobbing now, his shoulders shaking. "I'm sorry." The words wrenched from somewhere deep inside. "I'm so sorry. To all of you. To my family. To everyone I've hurt. I know it don't matter, I know it don't change anything, but I'm sorry."

No one responded. The apology hung in the air, inadequate and too late.

James stepped forward. "Mr. Benedetti, we're finished here. Deputies O'Brien and Peterson will transport you back to the holding cell. You'll be formally arraigned on Monday morning."

As the deputies moved to escort Sal from the room, he looked back one last time at the people who'd been his friends, his family, his whole world.

"Goodbye. And—and take care of each other. Don't let what I did poison everythin'. Joey's music—it was beautiful. Don't let my bitterness destroy that."

Then he was gone, led away in handcuffs, and the ballroom lapsed into heavy silence.

After a long moment, Kathleen stood. "I think—I think we should all go home. This has been too much for one day."

People rose and gathered their things. Vivian was still sniffling, supported by Molly on one side and Clarence on the other. The band members moved together, bound now by grief and the need to figure out what came next.

James appeared at my elbow, his expression weary but relieved. "It's over," he murmured. "Finally over."

"Yes." The last few people filed out of the ballroom. "Though I suspect the healing will take considerably longer than the investigation did."

"It always does." James took my hand, his thumb tracing gentle circles on my palm. "But justice has been served. That has to count for something."

"What will happen to him?"

"Depends on the prosecutor and the jury. If it's first-degree murder, he'll get life in prison if the judge is merciful, the hangman's noose if not. If they accept his claim that he didn't intend to kill Joey—manslaughter—more like ten to twenty years, possibly less with good behavior."

"Do you believe him? That he didn't intend to kill?"

"I think *he* believes it. Whether the jury will is another matter." He slid his arm around my shoulder and pulled me close. "That's for the court to decide. My job was to find the truth and bring the killer to justice. That's done."

We stood together in the now-empty ballroom, the afternoon light slanting through the tall windows and casting long shadows across the polished floor. The investigation was over, the killer had confessed, and justice would take its course.

But the reckoning—the real reckoning—was only just beginning.

Chapter Eighteen

The days following Sal's arrest passed in a strange, subdued haze. Timber Coulee seemed to hold its collective breath, coming to grips with the shock of another murder in their midst and the even greater shock of the killer's identity.

Sunday brought a development I hadn't anticipated. Reverend Miller devoted his entire sermon to the themes of judgment, mercy, and the human capacity for both good and evil.

"We are shaken this week by events that have touched our community deeply." His voice carried through the sanctuary. "A young man has died. Another young man has been revealed as his killer. It would be easy to simply condemn, to draw a line between the righteous and the wicked and place ourselves comfortably on one side."

He paused, his gaze sweeping across the congregation.

"But the gospel calls us to something more difficult. It calls us to recognize our own capacity for sin, our own vulnerability to jealousy, pride, and resentment. It calls us to mourn not only the victim but also the perpetrator—to grieve for what was lost in both men."

Several people around the sanctuary nodded. Even Martha Barrington, usually so quick to judgment, sat in her pew, her expression thoughtful rather than judgmental.

"Let us pray," Reverend Miller continued, "for Joseph Serpentine's soul, that he may rest in peace. Let us pray for Salvatore Benedetti, that he may find genuine repentance and, in time, God's mercy. And let us pray for ourselves—that we may have the wisdom to see our own failings, the courage to confront them, and the grace to extend compassion to others as we hope to receive it ourselves."

After the service, as Molly went to find Clarence and Kathleen and I filed out with the rest of the congregation, Martha Barrington approached.

"Miss Parrish." Her voice uncharacteristically subdued. "I owe you an apology. I was quite harsh in my judgments of you this week. I was wrong."

I nearly dropped my hymnal from the shock. "Thank you, Martha. That's very kind of you to say."

"Not kind. Simply honest." She adjusted her gloves with crisp efficiency. "I still think jazz music is unseemly, mind you. But I cannot deny that you handled this entire affair with remarkable discretion and intelligence."

It was perhaps the closest thing to high praise I'd ever receive from Martha Barrington, and I accepted it with as much grace as I could muster.

When Callan arrived at the shop on Monday morning, his usual taciturn expression was even more pronounced than usual.

"Heard they arrested that drummer fellow." He hung his coat on the rack by the door. "For murder."

"Yes." There seemed little else to say.

"Ne'er trust musicians." His tone held more sadness than I-told-you-so. "Too much passion, not enough sense."

"If we didn't trust musicians, we'd lose our entire clientele," I pointed out. But beyond that, I didn't argue. After the week we'd had, I was too tired for debate.

What surprised me, however, was the sudden surge in interest for jazz records. By noon, I'd sold more recordings of Paul Whiteman, King Oliver, and Louis Armstrong than I had in the previous three months combined.

"Morbid curiosity." Callan watched me wrap yet another purchase. "People want to understand what all the fuss was about. Why a man would kill o'er such noise."

But I suspected it was something more than morbid curiosity. Perhaps it was the town's way of honoring Joey's talent, of acknowledging that something beautiful had been lost. Or perhaps, after witnessing such tragedy, people wanted to understand what had driven men to such passion—both creative and destructive.

Moxie, for his part, had taken up permanent residence in the shop's front window, basking in what I could only describe as smug satisfaction. Every time a customer mentioned the murder or praised my role in solving it, the cat would stretch in a languorous manner, as if accepting personal credit for the entire investigation.

"That cat's gettin' too big for his britches," Callan observed, watching Moxie preen in the window. "Next he'll be wantin' a salary."

"He earned it. Without him, we might never have found the evidence."

Callan harrumphed, but said nothing more. Even his legendary resistance to change seemed muted in the face of recent events.

Monday afternoon brought unexpected visitors to Mountain Melodies. Sweet Lou Lancaster entered the shop with Norman and Frank in tow, all three looking considerably more composed than when I'd last seen them in the hotel ballroom.

"Miss Parrish." Sweet Lou removed his hat. "We wanted to thank you and the sheriff and everybody for gettin' the straight goods on Joey's death, even though the truth is hard to stomach."

"I'm sorry it had to be Sal." I meant every word. "I know how close you all were."

"We've been talking," Norman said, gesturing to his bandmates. "About what to do next. We can't just leave Timber Coulee and pretend none of this happened. Joey deserves better than that."

"We've decided to stay," Frank added. "To open that club Joey was talking about. Make it real."

Sweet Lou stepped forward, his expression earnest. "We found a property on Second Street—used to be a warehouse, but it's got good bones.

High ceilin's, plenty of space for a stage and a dance floor. The owner's willin' to lease it to us at a reasonable rate."

"That's wonderful. Joey would have loved that."

"We're calling it 'Joey's Place,'" Norman said. "Seemed fitting. A memorial to his talent and his dreams. A nice place, not a gin mill."

"We were hopin'," Sweet Lou continued, "that you might help us with the musical side of things. Get us records to study, give us a line on what the local folks might want to hear. You got a good sense of this town and its people."

"I'd be honored." The prospect of helping build something positive from such tragedy felt like a small redemption.

"And Miss Ashford," Frank said. "Vivian. She's still planning to go to teachers' college in Lewiston, but she mentioned she'd like to sing with us on weekends. If—if that's all right with everyone."

"More than all right," Sweet Lou said. "That girl's got a fine voice, and she loved Joey genuinely. We'd be proud to have her be our canary."

"And she's got nice gams, too," Frank blurted, then blushed.

I hesitated, turning over an idea that had been forming in my mind. "May I make a suggestion? It might seem unusual at first, but I think it could benefit everyone involved."

The three men exchanged curious glances. "Go on," Sweet Lou said.

"You know Ezra Coldwell? He runs the social dance academy over on Pine Street."

Norman nodded. "Heard of him. Teaches the traditional ballroom dances, sponsors those Fortnightly events for the young folks."

"Exactly." I chose my words carefully. "Mr. Coldwell has done wonderful work in this community for years. Parents trust him. The young people respect him. But..." I paused, weighing how frank to be. "His business has been struggling lately. Young people are excited about jazz, about the newer dances—the Turkey Trot, the Castle Walk. Mr. Coldwell doesn't know those styles, and I suspect he's worried about losing relevance."

"You think he'd see us as competition," Sweet Lou said.

"I think he might have already," I admitted. "When word got around about Joey's plans for a club, I noticed Mr. Coldwell seemed... concerned. But what if it didn't have to be competition? What if you could work together instead?"

Frank frowned, clearly puzzled. "How would that work? We're planning a jazz club, not a dance academy."

"Think about it." I warmed to the idea as I spoke. "You have the musical knowledge, the modern repertoire, the excitement that draws young people. Mr. Coldwell has the community's trust, years of teaching experience, and a reputation for running wholesome, well-chaperoned events. If you combined forces somehow—perhaps he could teach dance lessons at your club, or you could provide the music for his Fortnightly dances—"

"We'd have legitimacy," Norman finished, understanding dawning in his eyes. "Parents wouldn't worry so much about their kids going to a jazz club if Ezra Coldwell's name was attached to it."

"And he'd stay relevant," Sweet Lou added. "He could crib the new dances from us, start to teach them himself. Give his business a boost along with ours."

"It's just a thought," I said quickly. "I don't know Mr. Coldwell well—we're both in the Chamber of Commerce, but we've never been more than acquaintances. He's quite formal, rather traditional in his ways. He might not be receptive to the idea at all."

"But it's worth explorin'." Sweet Lou's expression brightened. "We want Joey's Place to be a respectable establishment, not some back-alley speakeasy. If workin' with Mr. Coldwell could help us win folks over..."

"And help the young people of Timber Coulee," I added. "They deserve good, wholesome entertainment that doesn't require them to choose between what's exciting and what's approved of. Maybe they could have both."

Norman grinned. "Joey would have liked that. He was always saying jazz wasn't something to be afraid of, that it could bring people together."

"Would you be willing to introduce us to Mr. Coldwell?" Frank asked. "Might help if the suggestion came from someone he knows, even a little."

"I could arrange a meeting." I was already mentally composing what I might say to Ezra. "Though I should warn you—this week has been difficult for everyone in Timber Coulee. The murder, the investigation... Mr. Coldwell might need some time before he's ready to think about business ventures."

"We ain't in a rush," Sweet Lou assured me. "We need to get the property lease finalized, start makin' over the warehouse. It'll be a few weeks at least 'fore we're ready to open. But if you could plant the seed with him, let him know we'd be interested in talkin'..."

"I'll speak with him. But I can't guarantee anything. This would be quite a departure from his usual way of doing things."

"We understand," Norman said. "But even if it doesn't work out, we appreciate you thinking of it. Shows you care about more than just solving the mystery—you care about what happens to this town afterward."

As the men left to continue their planning, I a small spark of hope kindled even brighter in my chest. Out of tragedy and loss, something new was being born. The music would continue, transformed but not silenced. And if I could help bridge the gap between tradition and innovation, between Ezra Coldwell's respectable past and the bandmates' jazzy future, perhaps Timber Coulee itself might find a way to move forward.

I made a mental note to speak with Ezra within the week. The conversation would require tact and diplomacy—qualities I'd been forced to develop over the past few days. If I could convince him to at least consider the possibility, the benefits could ripple through the entire community.

Sometimes, I reflected as I returned to organizing the new shipment of sheet music, the greatest mysteries weren't about who committed a crime, but about how people could come together afterward to build something better than what had been broken.

That evening, we gathered at my house for dinner—a quiet affair, just Kathleen, Molly, Clarence, James, and myself. The contrast to the chaotic dinner party with the Midnight Serpents couldn't have been more stark.

"I've been thinking," Kathleen said as she served the roast chicken, "about what Reverend Miller said on Sunday. About judgment and mercy and seeing our own failings."

She set down the serving platter and looked at Molly with an expression I'd rarely seen on my sister—one of genuine humility.

"Molly, dear, I owe you an apology. I've been so focused on teaching you to be a proper wife that I failed to see you already possess the most important qualities—kindness, intelligence, loyalty. You don't need me to make you ready for marriage. You already are. You'll make a wonderful home for Clarence, not because I taught you how to hem a napkin, but because you have a good heart."

Molly's eyes filled with tears. "Oh, Mother, that means more to me than you know."

"And," Kathleen turned to Clarence, "I owe you an apology as well. I judged you unfairly based on my own narrow understanding of what makes a good husband. But this week has shown me that character matters more than profession, and you, Mr. Butterworth, have shown remarkable character."

Clarence looked uncomfortable with the praise but managed a gracious, "Thank you, ma'am. That's very kind."

As dinner progressed, I watched the easy affection between Molly and Clarence, the way my sister had relaxed into a maternal warmth I'd never seen before, and thanked the Lord that some good had come from the terrible events of the past week.

After dinner, as Clarence and Molly cleared the dishes, Kathleen pulled me aside.

"You were right about the jazz music, about young people needing to make their own choices, about not judging what we don't understand. I've been so afraid of change that I forgot to trust the people closest to me."

"You were trying to protect what you love," I replied. "That's not wrong, Kathleen. You just needed to learn that the world can change and still be good."

"I'm learning." She gave a small smile. "Slowly, perhaps, but I'm learning."

By Tuesday, life in Timber Coulee had returned to something approximating normal. The shock had faded to a dull ache, the gossip had moved on to other topics, and the daily rhythms of small-town life had reasserted themselves.

At Mountain Melodies, I was restocking the jazz section—now significantly depleted thanks to the weekend's sales—when James appeared in the doorway.

"Thought I'd find you here." His eyes were bright, but his smile was tired. "Do you have a few minutes?"

"Always." I set down the records. "How are you holding up?"

"Exhausted. The paperwork alone is staggering. But the case is solid. Sal's confession, the physical evidence, the timeline—the prosecutor is confident we'll get a conviction."

"How is Sal?"

"Resigned, mostly. Almost peaceful, in a strange way. Like confessing lifted a burden he'd been carrying." James moved closer, his voice dropping. "But I didn't come here to talk about the case. I came to talk about us."

My heart quickened. "Us?"

"I've been thinking about what happened with Deputy O'Brien. About how I failed to see what was happening, failed to set proper boundaries. I never want you to doubt my commitment to you, Amanda. Not for a moment."

"I know. I trust you, James. And I'm sorry I let my insecurity get the better of me."

"You had every right to your feelings." He took my hand. "But I want you to be certain—absolutely certain—that there's no one else for me. There's only you. There's only ever been you, from the moment I realized what we could be together."

The declaration hung in the air between us, weighty with promise.

"I know we're taking things slowly," James continued. "I know you value your independence, and I respect that more than you know. But I want you to understand that my heart is yours. Completely."

I reached up to cup his face. The slight stubble on his jaw rough against my palm, the absolute sincerity in his eyes... they did delicious things inside of me. "I am certain," I whispered. "And I'm grateful—for your patience, for your partnership, for everything you are."

He smiled then, that rare, genuine smile that transformed his whole face. "We make a good team, Sheriff Holcomb and Miss Parrish."

"The best team."

The moment was interrupted by Moxie leaping onto the counter between us, howling as if to remind us of his crucial role in recent events.

James laughed, scratching the cat behind the ears. "And of course, our finest investigator. Can't forget Moxie."

"He certainly won't let us," I said in a dry tone.

As James prepared to leave—duty calling him back to the office—he paused at the door. "There's a town social on Saturday night. Nothing fancy, just dancing and refreshments at the community hall. Would you like to go with me? Officially, as my—" He hesitated, searching for the right word.

"As your sweetheart?" I suggested with a smile.

"Yes." His expression warmed, something almost sultry gleaming in his eyes. "As my sweetheart."

"I'd be delighted, Sheriff Holcomb."

After he left, I watched dust motes dance in the afternoon sunlight streaming through in the shop's window. Moxie stretched luxuriously on the counter, purring with satisfaction.

"Yes, yes. You're very clever. You found the evidence. You're the hero of the hour."

The cat's purr grew louder, and I couldn't help but laugh.

Timber Coulee continued its daily life. The tragedy of Joey's death would not be forgotten, but neither would it define us. The band would build their club. Vivian would pursue her dreams of teaching, strengthened rather than broken by what she'd endured. Molly and Clarence would marry and build their life together. Kathleen would continue to grow and change, learning to embrace rather than fear the new.

And James and I—we would continue to build whatever this partnership was becoming. Something stronger than friendship, deeper than professional collaboration, more enduring than romance alone. But a little romance wouldn't be bad either.

The music hadn't stopped. It had simply changed its tune. And in the end, perhaps that was the most important lesson of all—that life continues, that people adapt, that love and hope and resilience can grow even in the shadow of tragedy.

Moxie meowed again, demanding attention, and I obliged with a scratch behind his ears.

"Come on, you ridiculous creature. Let's close up shop and go home. We've earned our rest."

As I locked the door and turned toward home, I heard it—faint but unmistakable. The sound of a trumpet, drifting from somewhere downtown. Norman or Sweet Lou, perhaps, practicing in their new space. The first notes of Joey's Place coming to life.

I smiled and walked on, Moxie trotting at my heels, both of us heading toward whatever the future held. The case was closed, justice was served, and tomorrow would bring new challenges and new possibilities.

But tonight, we had this—simple, sweet, and enough.

THE END

Author's Note

While *Snake in the Brass* is a work of fiction, a few real-life historical situations provided inspiration for this story.

The novel is set in 1920, the first year of nationwide Prohibition after ratification of the 18th Amendment to the U. S. Constitution, which prohibited the manufacture, sale, and transportation of alcohol. The references to speakeasies and bootlegging belong to this era. It was not uncommon for tavern-keepers to repurpose their facilities as ice cream parlors and soda fountains, which sometimes served as fronts for illegal alcohol sales.

Northern Idaho was well situated for scofflaws smuggling liquor across the Canadian border. A highly lucrative occupation, bootlegging attracted both men and women, but the women had an easier time of it, for several reasons. Some state laws made it illegal for male officials to frisk or search women, creating a legal shield that criminals exploited. Socially, according to lingering Victorian-era attitudes about female propriety and capability, it was not only insulting to accuse a "respectable" woman of committing a crime like bootlegging, but considered practically impossible. Women bootleggers, exploiting these attitudes, would hide bottles underneath their clothing or within their automobiles. smile sweetly at the guards, and sail on past. As law enforcement agencies wised up, they hired female agents like Deputy Margaret O'Brien to investigate women bootleggers.

1920 also marked the beginning of the "Jazz Age" (a term coined by F. Scott Fitzgerald). Jazz was controversial and considered scandalous by older generations. The conflict between Kathleen's traditional values and Molly's enthusiasm for jazz reflects real generational tensions of the era. Jazz was associated with disreputable nightlife and moral laxity in the minds of many Americans, particularly in small towns like Timber Coulee. At the same time, it signaled, fun, excitement, and freedom to a society emerging from the horrors of the Great War only recently ended. Other aftereffects of that war can be seen in Callan MacTavish, who exhibits signs of what was then called "shell shock" and today would be termed "post-traumatic stress disorder" or PTSD.

In Gratitude

To God be the glory.

I offer my deepest thanks to:

Pegg Thomas, editor extraordinaire and the lazy adverb's worst nightmare;

Anita Aurit, Terese Luikens, and Grace Robinson, eagle-eyed writing companions and cherished friends;

Linda Nelson, first reader and sparkling fountain of encouragement;

the women of the Thursday night Bible study at Kootenai Church;

and especially my husband, Thomas Leo, for his love, support, patience, and willingness to talk through things that never happened to people who don't exist.

And thanks to you, dear reader, for taking a chance on my book. Please visit my website at JenniferLamontLeo.com to sign up for my Reader Community or drop me a line. I'd love to hear from you!

Also by the author

The Corrigan Sisters Series
You're the Cream in My Coffee
Ain't Misbehavin'
Wrap Your Troubles in Dreams

The Windy City Hearts Series
Moondrop Miracle
The Rose Keeper
Love's Grand Sweet Song

The Music Shop Mysteries Series
Murder on a High note
Something Wicked This Way Hums
Snake in the Brass

What's the Buzz?

Reviews are pure gold to an author! If you enjoyed this book and want to help spread the word, post reviews in book-oriented websites like Goodreads, Amazon, and Bookbub. Reviews can be short or as long as you like. And please talk about the book, in person and on social media. Word-of-mouth is still the best way to promote just about anything!

Let's stay in touch. Please stop by and say hello.

* Visit JenniferLamontLeo.com, where you can join my Reader Community for book news, exclusive content, and more.

* Look for me on social media.

* Listen to my podcast, A Sparkling Vintage Life, at sparklingvintagelife.com or subscribe in your favorite podcast app.